SEND NO
ANGEL

ISBN: 978-0-9839069-4-0

Cover Concept, Artwork and Design: JH Glaze
Text Editing: Susan Grimm
First Printing April 2013
Published by MostCool Media Inc.
"Make it interesting. Make it MostCool."

Proudly printed in the United States of America.

First Edition April 2013

10 9 8 7 6 5 4 3 2 1

Dedicated to Susan, my editor, my wife, my life. Without you I couldn't do this.

To my readers who give me the opportunity to entertain them every time I write yet another story. Your continued support means more to me than you will ever know.

To my Street Team: The J. H. Glaze Paranormal Warriors, you are some of the best friends and fans a writer could have.

Finally, thank you to all of those who listen to me every day as I go on and on about my next story. I have to admit, it really helps to talk about it and I'm not sorry I do it, I am just sorry you have to suffer through it.

Send No Angel

The Paranormal Adventures of John Hazard Book III

"Maybe this world is another planet's hell."

Aldous Huxley

One

It was 4:30 a.m., and he was the last one to leave the Players Lounge. He locked the front door on the way out, and walked around back to double check that the door in the rear of the club was secure. Emerging from behind the building, he held a handful of empty beer bottles, one dangling from each finger. He opened the gate to the fenced-in dumpster, and seconds later there was a clanging *thunk* of glass against metal. Silently, he closed the gate behind him and walked to his car. The alley was dark and empty as he drove off toward his home and some much needed sleep.

Archer sat sipping a cold cup of coffee as he took in the scene from his Ford pickup a short distance down the block. He had been waiting about an hour and a half for this moment and was relieved that soon he would be finished and on his way. He checked his mirror for any sign of activity. Picking up his tool bag, he stepped out into the street. There was little traffic in this part of town, especially at this hour. Casually, he walked up to the building and around to the back door, which was barred and secured with a heavy-duty padlock. He scratched his chin, trying to determine what he would need from his bag of tricks to gain access.

Instinctively, he reached for the pry bar, but thought better of it as he recalled that John had asked him to make what he was about to do look like an accident. He dropped the bar back into the bag, and instead fetched the lock picking kit from the inner breast pocket of his jacket. With a quick glance at his watch, he opened the small black case and selected one of the slim rods. He chose a second, tool with a flat end, then closed the case and set it on top of his bag.

Archer laughed as he spotted the familiar logo boldly proclaiming the quality of the lock. Pushing the thin rod into the keyhole on the bottom, he challenged, "Yeah, who's your Master?" He smiled to himself as he slid the second tool into the slot. Holding the first rod steady, he turned the flatter one like a key and the hasp popped out of the hole.

"Note to self," he muttered, "anything but a piece of crap like this to protect my shit." He worked it off the door and laid it on the ground. Pulling the bar to the left, he lifted it out of the u-shaped bolts that had held it in place and laid it next to the lock. The door had a conventional deadbolt so he retrieved his kit and swapped out the flat tool for something more appropriate. He was particular about organization in his bag, making sure to place the tool case neatly in its place on top of the bag before setting to work on the deadbolt.

"Fuckin' deadbolts," he scowled as he worked the tools into the keyhole. For the criminally inclined, the problem with deadbolt locks was that often they were not well maintained. It was better when they were lubricated occasionally, otherwise they could become quite sticky. This one was stuck tight.

He had prepared for this possibility, however. It was exactly the reason he had brought a tiny can of spray graphite. He inserted the thin red plastic tube into the hole and gave it a quick spray. For extra measure, he shot a stream behind the metal faceplate covering the bolt itself and managed to hit the bolt with enough of the slick powder to do the job.

Carefully returning the can to the bag, he went back to work on the lock. This time it turned easily, and he heard the satisfying click that signaled success. Archer made sure that everything was properly placed in the bag before taking a pair of rubber gloves from his pocket. He grimaced as he pulled them on and grabbed the doorknob to open it. Some folks like to wear leather or rubber gloves to prevent fingerprints, but he had a problem with sweaty hands and hated gloves of any kind.

He gave the knob a turn and stepped through the doorway into a very short hallway. To his right was a coat rack that had been screwed into the wall. It was hung full of dirty aprons and sweaters likely used by the female employees when the air conditioning got to be too much for them. To his left was a tiny utility room with mops and brooms, various types of cleaning products, and a yellow bucket on wheels next to the sink.

Just a short distance down the hall was the kitchen area. A lot of nightclubs didn't have a kitchen anymore, but this one opened each afternoon just in time for the day shift from surrounding warehouses and businesses to stop in for a cold beer and a sandwich before heading home. It made sense that food here was a good source of revenue.

Two small fluorescent lamps along the walls cast ample light throughout the room, enabling him to see quite clearly. Archer was sure he would not need his flashlight for this job. In the center of the room was an eight-foot, two-tiered stainless steel table covered with kitchen tools and neatly stacked square metal pans. To the right of the table was a counter along one wall, probably where the line cook or the wait staff assembled the salads, or did some of the prep work. Pushed against the wall were multiple bottles of ketchup, hot sauce, and some nasty looking bottles of mustard.

Archer wasn't interested in any of it. He looked to his left and spotted what he was hoping to find. A large gas-fired grill, and two greasy fryers that appeared to be cooling down as the congealed fat left trails around the large vats.

Quietly, he moved to the grill and squatted down to inspect its design. Excellent. It was an older model with a removable front panel providing easy access to re-light the pilot lights that were always burning just below the stainless burners. Except for the grease that had dripped down the front of this unit, it would be simple enough to accomplish what he intended.

***

On the other side of town, Joe stood behind the Uptown Grill and Bar staring at a circular lock on a bar across the back door of the Ambassador Lounge. This could be a problem. For an entire day, he had been given lessons on lock picking with the tool kit he now carried in his pocket. It had surprised him that he was such a natural when it came to opening all the various types of padlocks that had been included in his training. Unfortunately, none of his training had included the exact type of lock he was facing here. It had an unusual slot, round. It looked like an O with a post in the center. Sure, he had seen this type before on vending machines and whatnot, but he had no idea how to open it.

Not one to give up easily, Joe pulled the small black toolkit from his back pocket and opened it. Staring at it for a moment, he finally decided on the slim rod with the flat end. He pulled it out and put the case back into his pocket. With the lock in hand, he pushed the tool into the round slot and fished around for something that might release the hasp. He could feel where the key might fit into the tiny grooves cut into the moving parts inside, but even when he could get some leverage, the lock would not budge.

Assuming he had not given it enough muscle, he pushed harder.

Snap! The tool broke off in the slot. "Man, this is bullshit!" He threw the broken tool over the fence that stretched across the back of the lot. With a twinge of regret, he wondered if his fingerprints could be lifted from something that small. As tight as he had been gripping it, he would have left a partial print at least. No, his mind was messing with him, and this was no time to get distracted.

John was counting on him. He had a mission to complete. He knelt down and unzipped his bag. Blindly digging around, he pulled out a small sledgehammer. He took hold of the handle with both hands and planted his feet in a good wide stance. *Wham!* He hit the lock dead on.

"Fuck!"

The lock was still hanging there. Again, Joe pulled back and swung hard yet there it was, still intact. He was making far more noise than he should without getting any result. Archer had gone over padlock after padlock with him. At the end of the day, he'd been sure he was ready for anything. Then this shit is hanging here like nothing he'd seen. He stuffed the hammer back in the bag and zipped it up. "Time for Plan B!" he muttered as he walked back to his car some fifty yards away. Crossing the street, he checked both ways to make sure that no one would catch a glimpse of what he was about to do.

Two

Archer squatted in front of the grill to get a closer look at the grease-covered plate. He would have to remove it to get to the guts inside. Grabbing hold of each side, he pulled up with some force. Regrettably, the glove he was wearing slipped on the greasy surface and his hand slammed upward into the overhang of the grill above. "Shit!" Shaking his hand to distract from the pain, sweat dripped out of the glove and down his arm.

Slipping out of the glove for a moment, he reached into the bag and pulled out a round metal rod that was about eight inches long and made from solid iron. Three taps on the plate and out it came, popping up and falling to the floor with a loud clang. Although he saw it coming, he literally jumped at the noise. Every sound echoed against the contrasting silence of the closed building. Even the clink of the rod on the floor seemed loud.

Rummaging around in the bag again, his fingers recognized the slim flashlight and he clicked it on as he pulled it out. The bright LED light washed over the interior of the grill. He could see his target, the pipe that feeds the gas.

"Eureka!"

Like a miner who had just discovered a nugget of gold, Archer smiled wide as he uttered the word. He located the pilot light, its tiny flame glowing orange and blue in the darkness. Though it didn't look like much, he would have to extinguish it before he took the next step. He put his face close to the front of the grill and sucked in as much air as possible before he blew as hard as he could. Disappointed, he could see that it was still burning. Sucking in a big breath, he tried again, but there it was, still burning.

Reaching over to drag the bag a little closer, he groped around until he felt the cool metal surface of the can. He closed his fingers around it, pulling it from the bag. Taking the thin red plastic tube held snug against the can by a rubber band, he inserted it into the hole on the spray tip. He aimed the plastic tube at the pilot light and pressed the can of pressurized air up against the grill. He gave the small white button on the top of the can some pressure and watched as the flame blew out. He waited a second to make sure it was extinguished before putting the can back in the bag. As he turned back to face the grill, he realized that the flame was burning again.

"Shit!"

It was then that he saw the problem. There was a thin wire attached to a tiny metal rod above the flame. Glowing red, the wire was hot enough to reignite the pilot. It was going to take more than a shot of air to put this out. He took the can and flipped it upside down to shoot again at the flame. This time a small amount of liquid sprayed from the tube and cooled the rod as the flame was finally extinguished.

With the pilot light disabled, he could get on with his work. He picked up the metal rod he had left on the floor and took a rag from his bag. He wrapped it around one end of the rod before pulling a small sledgehammer from the bag. Holding the wrapped end of the rod up to the half-inch pipe that led to the controls for the grill, he pulled back the hammer and gave the other end of the pipe a solid *whack*. Immediately he heard the telltale hissing sound and smelled the gas as it leaked out into the room.

Archer placed his tools back into the bag and pulled out a small plastic box with a toggle switch. He flipped the switch and the small red light on the side of the box lit up. On top of the box was an igniter for a model rocket. It had been modified for just this purpose, connected to a remote switch and to the batteries that would fire it up. He zipped up his bag, stood and walked around the stainless table to the counter on the other side of the room and placed the box there. All he had to do now was to wait for the gas to fill the room.

Three

Across the street from the Uptown Bar and Grill, Joe stood waiting. He was holding the five-gallon plastic gas can and beginning to think he might be in for a confrontation when a car rounded the corner and began to slow down in its approach. Rather than give the driver a chance to get a good look at his face, he turned away with the can shielded from view and waited for it to pass.

Joe knew where he was. This place was in the middle of a large industrial complex. With no one around, and in this neighborhood, he might as well have a target on his back. Rather than be caught by surprise without time to react, he fingered the pistol he had tucked into his belt. He could feel his adrenalin begin to do its job. After a few tense seconds, the car continued down the street, accelerating to a normal speed as it moved further away.

"Son of a bitch! Don't be comin' back here. I ain't got time to be playin' right now." He was talking to tail lights as the car sped out of sight.

He crossed the street and headed to the back of the building. When he reached the bag he had left behind, he unzipped it and hastily pulled out a hammer, then zipped it back up and set it farther away from the building. He unscrewed the cap of the gas can, put the plastic seal in his pocket, and pulled out the eight-inch nozzle. Flipping it over, he replaced the cap to hold it in place, screwing it down tight to avoid any spillage.

Joe felt good now. He was in his groove as he picked up the hammer and strolled over to the nearest window. In the dim light, he could see the crisscross of wires embedded in the panes to prevent anyone from breaking the glass and crawling through. He had no intention of breaking into the building here. He just needed a hole. He raised the hammer and swung toward the glass. The shattered bits of glass flew everywhere and he stood looking at a hole exactly the size of the hammer head punched through the wires. On the other side, he could see a urinal in the dim light. He had broken through to the bathroom.

Screwing up his face, he muttered, "Figures." Joe dropped the hammer and lifted the gas can up to the window. Inserting the spout through the hole, he counted to ten while it poured into the room. He lowered the gas can and moved to the second of the three windows at the rear of the building where he repeated the process. Smash, check, and pour. This time the room inside appeared to be an office with a desk and some filing cabinets.

The last window was more of a problem. After he had smashed a hole in the glass, he discovered what appeared to be another wall made of sheetrock. There was a three-inch gap between the window and the wall, and he hoped that what was behind the wall was the interior of the club itself. If so, he might be able to get some gasoline on the carpet or furniture to get the best result. He put the gas can on the ground and walked back to his bag. There was a heavy metal rod about a foot long that he had planned to use on the grill if things had gone as planned, but now he had a new purpose for this crude tool. He was glad he had brought it.

Back at the window, he picked up the hammer and inserted the rod through the hole in the glass. Pushing the rod up to the wall, he pulled back the hammer and gave it a whack. When the rod punched through easily, it slipped from his grip. He let out a loud "Shit!" It had embedded halfway into the wall, but at least it had not fallen into the narrow space inside.

Using the hammer to open a bigger hole in the window, Joe reached through the broken glass and pulled the rod from the wall leaving a small hole. He put his face up to the window to get a peek into the room on the other side of the wall. All he could make out was a red glow. This was hopeful. He assumed it was coming from the neon bar lights. When his eye adjusted to the dim light, he could see a couple of tables and chairs.

"Oh, yeah, I got this," Joe exhaled. He used the hammer to knock out a bigger hole in the sheetrock, then pulled his arm back and reached for the can of gas. Taking a moment to pour some gas between the walls, he nearly emptied the rest of the can through the hole into the room. He saved just enough gas for the outside of the building and dribbled it across the ground to create a sort of fuse. Now all he had to do was move the tool bag and empty gas can to a safer distance, light the gas on the ground, and walk away.

Four

Archer closed the door behind him as he left the building. He turned and sat his bag on the ground. He considered locking the deadbolt lock, but why bother? Choosing to put the bar back in place instead, he snapped on the padlock and picked up his bag again. Before crossing the street, he looked around to be sure there was no one around. He walked up the block to his truck where he would wait for the leaking gas to fill up the bar.

***

Joe pulled a box of wooden matches from his pocket. He'd always wanted to light a match and throw it down dramatically like in the movies, a scene that had become cliché when someone was about to burn something to the ground. This was his chance. He slid back the cover of the box and extracted one of the matches. Holding it between his fingers, he closed the box. The match head flared as he pulled it against the striker and tossed it tumbling in slow motion at the trail of gasoline he had poured across the ground.

Unfortunately, the burning match had extinguished by the time it hit the ground. He tried again, tossing it immediately after it lit. The flame went out again as it fell to the ground. Determined to get this party started, he stooped down and tried one more time from about a foot away. The third time was a charm, and this time the gasoline caught fire. The golden flames raced along the ground and up the side of the building.

***

Archer believed enough time had passed to allow the gas to fill the building. He reached across the seat to drag his bag closer and pulled out a small black box similar to the one he had left on the counter in the kitchen except this one had a small telescoping antenna. He pulled it out to full extension then flipped a toggle switch on the side of the box. A small green light lit up.

"Come on, baby, let's dance," he said as he flipped up the clear plastic cap covering a red button.

***

Joe wanted to be sure that the flames would follow the gas trail through the wall before he walked away and the *whoosh* from the other side confirmed it. He turned and hurried back to retrieve the gas can and the bag. *Wharoom!* The side of the building blew out toward him. The impact lifted him and sent him tumbling head over heels as bricks and chunks of wood pummeled him from behind. Flames shot out from the building and over his head as he landed in a heap next to the fence.

***

Archer pulled a gold-plated cross from inside his shirt and kissed it for luck, then let it fall to his chest as he pushed the button. There was a moment of hesitation then *whump-BOOM!* The building exploded into flame and splinters.

Bits of wood and brick rained down on the street around his truck. He smiled as he put it in gear and rolled slowly away trying to avoid the burning debris that covered the road. The last thing he needed right now was a tire blowing out. At the next block, he made a left turn toward the highway. Mission accomplished. Soon sirens would break the early morning silence.

***

Joe lay on the ground stunned, his ears ringing. For a minute, he was not quite sure where he was. Iraq? Was he hit by a mortar blast, an IED? Everything that had happened in the past two years faded into haze. Was it really a dream? He was back in the war zone and nearly blown to hell. No, that wasn't it. He was regaining his senses now.

"Fuck! I'm in Oakland! Two tours in hell and I almost get my ass blown off in Oakland, by me!" He chuckled and began to push himself off the ground. There was something hot on his leg as he stood himself up. He swayed a little. Looking down, he finally realized his pants were on fire! Since drop and roll was not an option, he tried putting it out with his hands. It was probably a splash of gasoline because the fire proved difficult to extinguish.

Quickly, he looked around for a solution. Good fortune had provided a large puddle of water next to the dumpster enclosure. Hobbling over to it as fast as he could, he lowered his body to sit down and immerse his burning leg as much as possible. He used his hands to splash the water over the fire until it was completely extinguished. The smell began to hit his sinuses. He had just used the distilled ooze of weeks of rotten bar trash to put out the fire. The smell was intense and he burped loudly as his gag reflex kicked in. It was all he could do to keep from throwing up.

Joe eased himself up from the ground, his leg stinging from the burns. He was able to walk back to his bag of tools and the empty gas can. Gingerly, he bent to pick them up before making his way back to his car. As he climbed behind the wheel, he felt as though someone had beaten him with a baseball bat. It seemed an arduous task just to lift his legs off the ground and into the car. He closed the door and put the key in the ignition. He laughed as he looked at the burning building and put the car in gear.

"I love it when a plan turns to shit," he said and pulled out into the empty street. In the distance, he could hear sirens as fire trucks raced toward their destination.

Five

Eight Days Earlier:

It had been only two days since Frank DeMint had found his friend, John Hazard, along with his fierce though petite companion, Emily Sparks. Frank had hired a chopper to look for John when the small plane carrying his friend and others from a community college had gone missing. After hours of searching the National Forest somewhere between Washington and Oregon, and on the verge of giving up, Frank had decided to expand the search area. He finally found them, deep in some shit in the middle of a clearing, about to be eaten by eight-foot tall alien creatures.

After a complicated rescue, the couple had been covertly transported to a local doctor to check for serious injuries. The group steered clear of any hospital, at John's insistence. They needed to avoid any probing questions from local authorities. Fortunately, they were patched up and given an all clear. Now they were walking up the short sidewalk to Frank's very large home. John and Emily were hand in hand, while Frank carried a rifle case and duffle bag. There were several cars parked in the circular driveway when they pulled up to the house.

"Looks like the boys have arrived." Frank fumbled with his bags as he reached for the doorknob, but John insisted on getting it for him. He pushed the large, heavy oak door open and they stepped into the spacious foyer. It seemed the sunshine had followed them in as it streaked through windows high above them. The entry to the home was sparsely decorated, but the bright light made it seem cheery despite its stark minimalism.

"What do you think John?" He wagged his head to invite them to look around the room. "I have this hot Japanese decorator, and she does the Feng Shui thing. She's a real professional too, if you catch my drift." He nudged John in the ribs.

"It's beautiful," answered Emily as she looked up at the large windows above the doorway.

"You probably didn't notice as you came in, but your personal energy was drawn into the room instead of rushing out the door." Frank smiled wide.

"Really, Frank?" John looked puzzled. "I didn't know you were all into that New Age stuff." His eyes focused on a large painting, and he cocked his head trying to figure out what it was.

"New Age, hell. This is ancient shit, John. It surprised the crap out of me how much better I felt after she had finished working on it." He laughed. "Cost me a pant load, too."

"Better as in…?" asked Emily. "I mean, considering she *is* a *real professional*."

"Well, for one, I felt like I had a lot more energy. It revved me up to do all kinds of things including showing some gratitude to my designer." He stopped and smiled again. "But seriously, it seemed like things were better somehow. I could think more clearly and any issues with my business were easier to resolve. Then…"

Frank was interrupted by a tall man entering the foyer. "Hey, guys. They're here. Looks like Feng Shui Frank here picked up a new trophy in Seattle." He scanned Emily from head to foot, pausing for an extra long look at her breasts. She gave him a stern look and shifted to stand closer to John.

"Hazard, my boy, you're still as ugly as ever!" The man stepped forward arms open wide. John did not seem surprised when he received a bear hug from the huge man.

Slapping the guy on the back, John replied, "Crazy Joe Landry. I see you still need glasses!"

The man eyed Emily again, and grinning like a Cheshire cat, nodded in her direction. "You gonna introduce me to the eye candy, John?"

"Emily, this is Crazy Joe, part of the crew I told you about from my time in Iraq."

"Well I guess that explains everything." Emily held out her hand to shake his. "Emily Sparks. Should I call you by your first name or your last, Mr. Joe?"

Joe took her tiny hand gently in his, bent over with puckered lips and kissed it. "Just Joe is fine, my lady." As he straightened, a broad toothy grin spread across his face. "But Crazy *is* what my friends call me."

"So the whole crew is here? I only saw a couple of cars in the driveway," Frank inquired.

"You know it, Frank. When you put out the word, we got right on it. Some of the guys rode here together to save some cash on gas." Joe turned and walked toward the large doorway ahead of them.

Six

In the living room, seven men sat deep in conversation as John and Emily entered behind Frank and Joe. Emily relaxed a little as she took in the scene. Although the room was spacious and had a vaulted ceiling, there was a cozy, yet masculine feel.

"Miss Emily is new to the team, so let's make it official." Frank pointed at the first man sitting on the large, overstuffed sectional sofa. "Max, you go first. Then we'll go around the room like some kind of support group or something."

Each man introduced himself, standing to shake her hand politely and then returned to his seat. When all were finished, she replied, "I'm Emily Sparks. It is definitely very nice to meet you all."

John stepped forward greeting each man with a hug and a back slap or two. "It's great to see you again." "You look good for an old guy." "Are you still living with that stripper?" It was the kind of conversation one could expect in a reunion of old friends.

"Great!" Frank clapped and rubbed his hands together. "Now let's get down to business." He motioned to John and Emily to sit in two unoccupied chairs that had been brought into the room from a dining room table. They gladly obliged as he took his seat at the end of the assembled group.

"I know you received a very cryptic invitation to this meeting, but when you hear John and Emily's story," he waved his hand toward the pair, "I'm sure you will agree that they are in need of an intervention. I believe we can help."

Joe spoke up, "What, you guys doing drugs or something'? Shit, John, I thought you were against all that, bein' a cop and…"

John cocked his head at Joe. It was hard to believe anyone would accuse him of anything to do with drugs, any of these guys especially. The expression on his face spoke volumes.

"No, that isn't the problem at all. Geezus," Frank interrupted, "You should know better, Joe. I think maybe I should let John and Emily tell you the story." He hesitated, "Before they get started I need to warn you, the shit they are going to share here has two caveats. One, no matter what they say, you cannot repeat it to anyone. B, as crazy as it's gonna sound, I can tell you I've seen it for myself, so I know it's true."

Paulie couldn't remain silent. "It's government cover up shit, isn't it? I told you guys they was covering up stuff. What did you find, John?"

The others were intent on getting to the issues. They were beginning to feel frustrated with Paulie. Frank had just opened his mouth to speak when Philip fired off, "Paulie, why does everything have to be a government conspiracy with you? Let them tell their story."

"Because most everything *is* a government conspiracy. You just gotta look around and see the signs." Paulie put his hands up next to his temples with index fingers pointing out from his eyes and looked around the room.

"He's right," Max interjected. "In fact, I saw a couple of signs on the way here today."

"See, I told ya!" Paulie felt vindicated.

"Right," Max continued, "There was a sign about a mortgage broker, one about the Birds of Paradise strip bar, and even..." he lowered his voice for effect, "even a stop sign. Holy shit! The government is definitely in on that one."

The other guys stifled their laughter, but it was Malcolm who blew out the water he was about to swallow. It went everywhere as he started choking and roaring with laughter. That was all it took to get the rest of them started.

A splotchy patch of red spread across Paulie's face. He was getting pissed. Clark kept a relatively straight face as he interrupted the group of chortling comrades. "Hey guys, lighten up. Paulie's right, there are more conspiracies out there than we can even imagine. What the hell do you think the CIA does all day, bake cookies?"

"Well, every time something weird happens..." Charles stood up, "Paulie has to go off on his conspiracy shit." He stepped over to a table where a plate of cookies awaited, picked one up and immediately shoved the whole thing in his mouth. "Know what I'm sayin?" He chewed a little longer, swallowed hard and exclaimed, "Damn! These are some good CIA cookies!" Crumbs flew from his mouth as he spoke.

Frank figured it was time to take control of the conversation. "Look, just give a listen, then you can decide for yourself. Go ahead, John."

Seven

John began to stand up. He looked over and smiled at Emily who was smiling back at him. He decided to sit down again while he told the story. Settling back into his chair, he ran his hand through his closely cropped hair and down the back of his neck before relaying the horrific events they had recently survived.

"I don't even know where to begin. The story I'm about to tell you will sound unbelievable, but please hear me out." He looked at Emily who was nodding encouragingly. "First, in case you haven't seen one for yourself, ghosts really do exist."

He paused expecting some kind of response, but the group sat stone-faced, as though they were waiting for the punch line. "Second, aliens are real." The room was silent.

Suddenly, Paulie jumped out of his chair "I fucking told you they was real! The government has been covering it up just like I said. Area 52, Broom Lake, that shit's real! Yeah John, tell it."

"Well, yes and no, Paulie. I mean I don't know anything about Area *51* or *Groom* Lake, but there was definitely zero government involvement where this was concerned."

Pausing again, he scanned their stunned faces before continuing, "However, we witnessed it first hand. There are genuine, giant, ugly, hungry aliens up in the National Forest and they are definitely *not* eating Reese's Pieces or trying to phone home."

"Come on, John. You expect us to believe that shit?" Max smiled. "This is a joke, right? Frank, you crazy bastard, bringin' us all here for a story like…"

"Max, guys, I wish I could just bust out laughing' right now, but this shit is for real. Show 'em your chest, John." He motioned John to pull up his shirt.

The gashes across his chest were swollen and red around the edges, but he had passed on the stitches when they checked him out at the medical center. "One of 'em clipped me when we were rolling around on the ground. I didn't even realize it until we were in the chopper. Considering what I saw those monsters do to the others we were with, I was the lucky one."

"Others?" Charles leaned in.

"Emily was there. She saw it all. They ate at least four or five of my friends." His gaze wandered off as he recalled the horror of it. "We're still not sure what happened to a couple of them. When we got split up, I'm guessing they were torn apart or eaten by the bastards. These things were relentless. We even saw them rip each other apart and eat their own. They were at least this fucking tall!" He held his hand a couple of feet above his head.

Emily could see the group was still incredulous. "Look, I know it sounds crazy. If I hadn't seen it, lived through it myself, I probably wouldn't believe it either. They pulled our plane right out of the sky. They glued us to the trees and tried to feed us to their damn babies. If it hadn't been for the fact that John had his knife on him when they captured us, we wouldn't be here right now."

Paulie saw a chance to say it one more time. "I told you it was real. Laugh at me now, motherfuckers. Hah! Go on, John. They were Grays, right, just like in them documentaries, but big ones." He stood up and looked at them for a nod of agreement.

"No, not gray." John took a moment before continuing, "They could change colors, but not enough to completely camouflage themselves. You could definitely see what was comin' to kill you, the bastards."

For the next hour or so, John and Emily filled the men in on as many details they could remember. Whenever John forgot something, Emily would fill in the gaps. Between the two of them, the group was getting the whole picture painted with enough color to make them sit listening slack jawed.

When they finally got to the part where Emily had stepped up to save John, an absolute hush fell across the room. Frank coughed just as Charles broke the silence. "Hot damn! Where can I find me a girl like that? Emily, you got any sisters?" She smiled and shook her head, no.

"I'd hang onto her if I were you, John. Most babes would have either made a dash to the chopper or just screamed while you fed the fucker with your sorry ass." Clark was giving Emily the once over as he spoke. Her expression seemed to go from relaxed and friendly to stern and no-thank-you as he finished his sentence.

"I think we'll hang together for a while, that is if she feels the same as I do. You don't tell a girl like *her* what's what, and that's how we likes it!" John was looking at her and grinning.

Clark nodded appreciatively. "So did you kill 'em all, or are they still up there? I mean… the aliens."

"Not sure. There were probably hundreds still alive when we got away, but then some were eating the others. Some came after us. We didn't kill very many."

Emily put her hand to her forehead. "To be honest, I really don't care as long as they do themselves in and we don't have to be there. In fact, I don't care if I ever set foot in a forest, any forest, again. I've had enough of the nature thing!"

Eight

There were numerous questions for John and Emily, and they answered them as best they could without exaggeration. They concluded the Q&A session with the series of events leading up to Emily joining John's class excursion to the Northwest, why she had participated even though she was not a student of paranormal investigation.

"And that, fellas, is why I called all of you here. We need to help John and Emily find a way out of Emily's predicament." Frank looked at the faces in the room, waiting for someone to speak.

"Let me get this straight," Max spoke first. "You went to the Players Lounge to apply for a job, witnessed some bastard getting shot in the head for God only knows what reason." He cleared his throat and continued, "Then while you were running away, you dropped your resumes, which meant they got hold of your address and everything. Is that right?"

"In hindsight maybe it's not such a good idea to put your address on a resume." Emily appeared a little forlorn.

Joe pried his way in, saying, "The Players Lounge is owned by some bad dudes. Houston, I think we really *do* have a problem."

"I know what you mean, Joe. I've heard stories. That's why we need your help. We could go to the cops and file a report, but there's a chance something bad could happen." John stared off into the other room as he tried to decide how to say what he was thinking without sounding completely paranoid.

How much more insane could it sound after he had just told a story about aliens eating his classmates, he wondered. "If we go to the cops, then we can't be sure who will handle the case. Chances are there will be some money floating around on the streets, some of it flowing into the pockets of a dirty cop, and nothing good would come of it except a kill order being put out on Em. I've been told that there are quite a few independent contractors on the streets both here and in Oakland."

"I've heard that shit. Ya see it on TV all the time. Guns for hire get the job done. Dirty cops look the other way. Not a good place to be." Paulie was not helping with his police drama comments. John shot him a look that shut him down.

"Or… the cops might launch an investigation, put her under police "protection" and we could end up with the same outcome." John hesitated, as he was about to suggest something that was opposed to everything he had ever stood for. "I hate to say it but…"

"I say kill 'em all and let God sort it out. It shouldn't take half a second. I got no problem with cleaning up the streets." It was as though Malcolm had read John's mind.

"I didn't know if I wanted to say it, Mal, but you're exactly right. We could threaten them, take a few of them out, but they would just hire more contractors to take us out. I can't see any other way to deal with this problem but to exterminate it, get rid of it permanently."

John stood and walked to the table where the plate of cookies sat and grabbed one. He turned with nervous energy and continued, "I don't like this idea one bit. I believe in the rule of law. Hell, I was a part of the justice system not that long ago. However, in this case, the only justice we are likely to get is the justice we deliver for ourselves."

"Good ole' Wild West justice. That's what I'm talkin' about. I'm in!" Charles exclaimed.

The room rang out with, "Count me in," "I got your back," and "Let's do this," until each one had an opportunity to speak.

"We oughta give ourselves some fake names for this here operation," Paulie added.

"I'll be Mr. White." Joe grinned, claiming his identity.

"More like Mr. Potato Head!" Clark howled while the others joined in the laughter. John waited while the joke ran its course before asking the obvious, "So we're all in?" Everyone nodded. "All right then, Marines. We've got ourselves a rat infestation. Let's build a trap and plan the extermination. Find me a place in this cabana where we can draw it up!"

Without any further hesitation, the classic Marine response echoed throughout the room, "Oorah!"

Nine

The plan was simple. They would manipulate the situation like a chess game, taking advantage of the oppositions' anger and fear and using it against them. They would create an incident, something big, and prey on the mistrust generated between the local gangs. In the end, it would bring most, if not all, of the players together in one location for their untimely demise.

Step 1: Agitation

The first move would be to create some situation that would infuriate the gang from their lowest levels right on up to the leadership. Several ideas were floated. Joe suggested finding the cars of gang members and blowing them up. He figured if they did that, then everybody involved would be ready to go at it.

However, Max countered, "If we blow up their cars, how are we gonna get 'em to drive to another location so we can wipe them out? You think they'll all just ride the bus? I don't think so!"

Phil thought they could kidnap some of their family members. "We could just pretend like we're kidnapping them. You know, pick the kids up at school, take 'em somewhere and hold 'em till we're finished. Then we let 'em go."

"Kidnapping? I don't think so. That would bring out the FBI. We won't do well with that kind of heat. Besides, I never want to involve kids, no matter who their parents are. No, it's got to be something that will begin and end with local authorities." John was familiar enough with local law enforcement since he had been on a small town force for some years. He suggested, "We want to make it look like a case of gang on gang violence that ultimately goes nowhere. We just need the right kind of incident to kick it off."

"What about the club?" Emily finally decided to speak out. "What if we burned it down?"

"Now there's a plan." John beamed with pride as he added, "If we hit the club, we can make it look like an accident. When the fire inspectors show up, they'll tag it as a grease fire or something. We just need to make sure it doesn't look like arson."

"Why not make it look like arson?" Charles was just walking back into the room after excusing himself to use the bathroom. "That kind of shit happens all the time in Gangsta Land. The cops'll just think it was another gang. Revenge, or just plain rivalry right?"

"Arson leads to a full investigation," Frank pointed out. "An investigation is the last thing we need."

"I've heard these guys have two clubs. One here and one in Oakland. We should hit both of them. That'll really piss them off." Malcolm waited for a response.

"Yeah… it will. Anybody got any objection to cutting off both legs?" John scanned the group, "All right then, we'll take down both clubs at the same time."

Ten

Step 2: Word on the street

"After we take down the clubs, we're gonna have to get the word out. We'll need some connection to the guys on the street who are hooked up to these assholes. Anybody have any ideas?"

"I got some connections that might work. There's some kids that hang down around the docks. They're always bragging about hows they can get me anything I need. They can probably get the word out with a few calls." Paulie was quick to step up. "I think I got this."

"Okay, Paulie. Anybody else?" John was pleased.

"I know some people who know some people." Malcolm volunteered. "When are we planning on doing this thing?"

"I figure it'll take about a week or so to put it all together. We have to get ourselves some tools and weapons. We need to figure out the final location, where we want this to play out, and get things set up. This plan is going to have to wipe out *all* of the leaders, or we'll be dealing with them again. It's gonna take more than a flaming closed sign on the clubs to bring out the big guys. They will have to be pressed to the point where they feel they need the satisfaction of killing someone themselves." John thought for a moment. "We gotta make it look like we're moving in on their territory."

***

Dressed in a tailored designer suit, the man appeared quite uncomfortable standing before the rough looking man behind the mahogany desk in the well-appointed office. They were somewhere on the west side of town.

"We got problem, dog face," said Dmitri, his accent always more pronounced when he was under pressure. Sitting behind the large desk, the San Francisco boss leaned forward with one fist clenched and the other pointing at the man in front of him. "That bitch came into club just as we put him down. She's gotta be back in town by now. We should find her soon as possible!"

"What makes you think she could be back? The news reports say those people are missing in the woods. The slut is probably dead already." The last thing Jerry needed was more trouble right now.

"Yeah, and news also give names of everyone missink. I did not see her name on list. You been watchink her apartment like I told you?" The boss was not in the mood for a wrong answer.

"Boss, I had my guys watchin' her apartment for almost two weeks now. She ain't been nowhere around it. I don't think she's comin' back. I mean, if I knew you was looking for me, I sure as fuck wouldn't come back around here."

Dmitri pushed his finger closer to Jerry. "You don't find her," he snarled, "then you better tink about move somewhere I can't find you. Everything was run smooth until she showed up. Now organization argue about who will take my place when I go to the prison." He slammed his fist on the desk.

"Boss, you ain't goin' to no prison! I'll find her if I has to go up into them woods and bring the body back myself."

"Listen what I say, asshole! The bitch not missink. Her name not on list. Meaning, she is back, and I want proof of her kill. I want her head!" Dmitri's face was red now. A blue vein pulsed near his temple.

Jerry was in a hurry to get out of the office before the boss put a bullet in his face. He was known for such irrational moves. In fact, it was how that guy, Tre, had ended up with a bullet in his skull at the club and a new mailing address at the city landfill.

"I guess I better go check on my guys, boss. See if they seen anything." Jerry started to turn toward the door.

"You get me that whore, Jerry," Dmitri growled, "or you gonna end up sharing a bed with Tre. You understand me?" He was stretched across the desk with his fist waving menacingly in the air.

"Yeah boss, I got this." He walked out of the office and closed the door behind him. Shaking his head, he leaned against the wall for a moment. His heart pounded in his chest. He knew his time was running out.

***

Step 3: Ambush

"I have weapons, John," Frank volunteered. "You may remember I've always been into firepower. You can see it in the games we've been developing for the past ten years or so."

"You mean the metal in the games is the kinda stuff you got?" Paulie's eyes lit up with interest. "I thought we were using toys for the video, boss."

"Seems like a good time for a bit of disclosure, guys. Follow me." Frank left the room with the group following behind him. "I always wanted to show you guys this, but I was waiting until my collection was better organized."

He led them down a hall to an oversized painting. It was an artistic depiction of some people involved in an outdoor activity, maybe a marketplace, or some kind of sporting event. Everyone was holding their hands, palm out toward the observer. It was a very large canvas and hung close against the wall, all the way to the floor. Frank placed his hand over one of the crudely rendered hands. From behind the painting, the whirring sounds of machinery could be heard and the painting pushed out from the wall about two inches. The sound of compressed air escaped as it slid to one side. A stunned look crossed each face as a wide metal door was fully exposed.

Frank smiled at them and said, "Biometric lock. Really cool tech, only the bio signal of those programmed into it will work." The painting clicked as it locked in the open position. "Cost a fucking fortune, but it's the best security money can buy."

He stepped forward as the metal door slid open giving them entry into an elevator, big enough for the entire group to comfortably fit inside. When everyone was in, the door slid shut as Frank uttered one word, "Armory."

The elevator responded with a female voice. "Yes, Frank. Are we having a good evening?"

"Certainly, Alice. Kicking ass and taking names as always."

"That's nice, Frank. The world needs a good ass-kicking every now and then."

After a few seconds the voice announced, "We've arrived at the armory. Have a wonderful evening, Frank."

"Thanks, Alice, you too," Frank replied as the sound of pressurized air gave a telltale *whoosh* and the door slid open.

"Fuckin' Alice?" Max said. "Where'd you get that name?"

"Housekeeper on the Brady Bunch. I always loved that show." Frank beamed one of his bright smiles as he stepped out of the elevator.

"I thought that voice sounded familiar," Emily whispered to John.

Frank continued down the hall and stopped at the first door on the left as the crew followed. Beyond that door appeared to be many similar doors, but it was hard to tell how many rooms there could be since the hallway rounded a corner. It looked like a hall from some upscale hotel. There were potted plants and plush carpeting throughout. Each door was adorned with a brass number.

The number on the door they were about to open was appropriate – 007. It was half again as wide as a standard door, and John figured it was made of very thick steel judging by the weight of the welds. To the right of the door was a slightly recessed panel on which Frank placed his hand saying, "The thing I like about these panels is that it doesn't matter how you position your hand. It'll even read it upside down."

The door did not swing or slide out. Instead, it moved entirely into the room, then slid to the left. It was about four inches of solid metal. Ordinary hinges could never have held that much weight. Frank stepped through as the lights in the room flickered on. With his usual sunny smile, he held his arms out to his sides and declared, "Welcome to the Armory!"

Eleven

A black SUV was parked on Rockland Street just down from Emily's vacant apartment. The two men inside were drinking coffee from heavy paper cups covered with foam sleeves. Their expressionless eyes zeroed in on an old brick front apartment building. Save for the classical music playing softly from the radio, they sat in near silence.

"Come on, Leo! How can you stand to listen to that shit all da time?" The smaller man sitting in the passenger seat addressed the baldheaded man behind the wheel.

"It's not shit, asshole. It's Pachelbel. It's beauteeful. I find it to be soothing."

"Soothing? It makes me feel like killing something."

Just then, his phone rang, the hip-hop ringtone singing out with lyrics about bitches and guns. He fumbled with his coffee while digging it out of his jacket pocket.

"Yo," he said into the mouthpiece. "Yeah… right. We got that… No, ain't seen the bitch… Wha?" The man on the other end of the call was angry, his voice growing louder by the second until even Leo could hear the last sentence quite clearly.

"I don't care what you gotta do or who you have to kill, the boss wants that bitch dead… today!" The words swirling out of the speaker on the phone hung in the air like morning fog as the call ended.

"Sheeiitt. Jerry sounded pissed," he said as he put the phone back in his pocket.

"Yeah, I heard. What'd he say we gotta do?" Leo pulled the keys from the ignition and shoved them in his pocket.

"He said to go all up in the building, get some people to talk and shit. Like, fuck 'em up if we have to." His face screwed up to form a question mark. "I don't get it. If we go in there and start beatin' down people..."

"Somebody's gonna call the cops. Right, but if we don't do it, sounds like the boss is gonna make us disappear!" Leo held his hands out from the steering wheel. "Alright, let's do this!" He glared at his partner until he reached for the door handle.

"Yeah, okay, right." Jackson opened the door. "I'll follow you."

The two men looked around cautiously as they crossed the street and approached the door to the building. All was clear except for a homeless guy digging through the trash. He reached out when he saw the men approaching and, with bloodshot eyes, he asked, "Can ya help a brotha with a dollar?"

Ignoring the bum, they climbed the steps to the door. They reached the uppermost step just as one of the residents left the building. Leo stepped out of the shadows and caught hold of the door before it closed, slipping through into the lower hallway with Jackson close behind. Once inside, they stood looking around at the mailboxes and apartment doors down the hall.

"You got the apartment number?" Leo asked.

"Shit, I thought you had it"

"Go back out to the truck and get it. Damn! I'll wait here." He turned and leaned against the wall.

"I got a better idea," Jackson replied. "Her name is Sparks, right?"

"Yeah." Leo was reading a text message on his phone. He began typing furiously in response, sniping, "Damn women. Can't do nothin' without a credit card and a shitload of instructions."

"I think we can find her over there." Jackson pointed at a row of metal mailboxes built into the wall to their left. He walked over and ran his finger along them as he searched for the name. "Got it," he announced tapping the label on the mailbox. He turned and smiled, "Follow me."

He moved to the stairs and began climbing with Leo following directly behind him. As they reached the landing, they went straight to Emily's apartment.

"Allow me," said Leo as he pushed Jackson to one side. Stepping up to the door and putting his ear to it, he held his breath and listened.

After a moment, he looked over at his partner and shook his head, "I don't hear nobody." He took hold of the knob and twisted it only to find that it was unlocked. Stunned, he cautiously opened the door.

Jackson reached into his jacket and pulled his gun from the shoulder holster, readying it for any surprise they might encounter. The apartment was messy, but looked untouched for having sat empty and unlocked for more than a week. By now, it might have been ransacked, but nothing looked out of place. "She ain't here," he said to Leo.

"Like I'm blind and couldn't see that, you mook?" Leo had been opening closets and checking the bathroom, but now stood in the middle of the living room, his gun in his hand.

"I'se just sayin." Jackson waited to see what Leo wanted to do next.

"Okay, it don't look like she's been here either. Time to talk to some neighbors."

He turned and headed out the door with Jackson following behind. First, he eyed the apartment just across from Emily's, then the next one down the hall.

"Let's pay this one a visit." Leo nodded across the hall, and stepped up to the door. From outside they could hear a woman's voice. It sounded to Leo like she was having a conversation with someone else in the room, so he decided not to kick the door open as he had planned. Instead, he banged on the door.

A few seconds later, someone on the other side unlocked several locks before opening the door as far as the chained lock would allow. Standing in front of the gap in the door was a short old woman holding her cat. She blinked and squinted at the two men before a very large smile spread across her face.

"Bobby! You finally came to visit after all these years," she beamed. "I was afraid that mother of yours would never let me see you again. And you brought Timmy with you too!"

She put down her cat, unchained the door, and opened it to hug Leo, burying her face in his chest. He stood there speechless for a moment. This was not what he had expected. Her hair smelled a little musty, and he turned his head to one side to avoid the funk.

Finally, she stepped back and apologized, "Oh boys, what was I thinking? I'm sorry, do come in." Her small wrinkled hand reached out for Leo's arm and she tugged him through the doorway.

"Uh, we wanted to ask you about your neighbor…"

The two men stood just inside the door. Jackson waved toward Emily's apartment. "Sparks. The one across the hall."

"Of course. Boys, sit down. You must be starving. Let me get you some cookies and milk." She shuffled toward the kitchen. The scent of cat litter was so strong that it made the men feel a little queasy.

"We ain't really hungry, ma'am," Leo called after her. She didn't seem to hear. He turned to his partner. Pinching his nose to make a face, he tilted his head toward the door.

In a hushed voice Jackson implored, "I'm kinda hungry, boss. Cookies sound real good." He cleared his throat and shouted into the kitchen, "What kinda cookies you got, granny?"

The woman was already headed back with a large silver tray loaded with cookies. There were a couple of napkins and two large glasses of milk.

"Why, it's Bobby's favorite." The two men looked at each other quizzically. "You remember, Bobby, chocolate chip cookies freshly baked."

She reached the table where she placed the tray directly in front of the sofa. "You boys shouldn't eat standing up. Help yourself. Take a seat on the sofa." She looked at them expectantly. "Come on now, be good boys."

Jackson nudged Leo with his elbow. "Come on, Boss. We got a minute. Those cookies are calling my name. My ol' lady never makes shit like that. I gotta eat 'em out of a box all da time."

"Okay, okay. I might be able to do a coupl'a cookies." They each took two cookies and a napkin and obediently moved to sit on the sofa.

"That's some good boys," she said.

She left the tray of cookies and milk and headed back into the kitchen. Leo tried holding his breath in order to enjoy the fresh baked treat. Suddenly he noticed that there were several cats sitting, sleeping and walking around quietly throughout the apartment. It could have been as many as twelve or more. No wonder the place smelled so bad.

"You sure got lots of cats, lady," he yelled back to the kitchen.

The old woman was drying her hands on a small towel as she shuffled her way back into the living room. "Oh yes, I just love cats," she said in a musical voice. "They're such wonderful friends and so smart! I think they sense all kinds of things that people can't."

She sat down in the frayed armchair across from the sofa. At once, a tabby jumped up on her lap while a small black cat curled up behind her on the top back of the chair. "Go on now. I know you are hungry."

They looked at each other, shrugged their shoulders, and grabbed a couple more cookies. As he swallowed the last bite, Leo reached for his milk and greedily gulped half the glass as Jackson shoved another whole cookie into his mouth.

"That's some good boys," she said again. "I knew you must be starving after sitting out there in that truck all day." Leo nearly choked as he tried to clear his mouth to speak, "You been watchin' us, lady?"

"Oh, not watching you, exactly. I look out my window every so often, and I could see you out there, just sitting there. It must be a tiresome day just sitting and watching. Are you boys policemen?"

Leo regained his composure. "Nah, nuttin' like that. We're, uh, part of the Neighborhood Watch. We're lookin' out for bad guys." He forced a smile revealing chocolate chip smudges on his yellowed teeth.

"How nice. It's comforting to know that someone is keeping an eye on the neighborhood. Go on now, dear, have some more cookies."

Jackson took another look around the apartment. Something didn't seem quite right. There were way too many cats, and even more coming and going from the other rooms. Here's an old lady, feeding them milk and cookies, calling them by some strange names yet obviously aware that they had been watching the place all day.

In a sudden flash, a vision perhaps, he saw himself and Leo clutching their throats, falling to their knees on the floor. All at once, he felt himself floating above the kitchen while Leo lay on a plastic covered table, his arm sawn off and lying on the floor. A multitude of cats, all sizes and colors, surrounded the amputated limb, lapping at the blood as it dripped from the table.

In his daymare, he caught a glimpse of the old woman who was whistling a tune as she went to the refrigerator and opened the door. Inside was a single shelf set above a limbless bloody, naked torso. On the shelf above the torso, to his horror, was his own severed head, frozen in a startled expression staring lifelessly out at the carnage.

"Aaaaargh!" he cried out as he snapped back to reality and choked on the cookie in his mouth. The old woman's smile faded as she was startled by the sound.

"Are you okay, son?" she asked as she stood to help him. "I hope you didn't choke on my cookies."

"Boss, we gotta get the fuck outta here. Now!" Jackson abruptly stood up, knocking over the glass of milk that he had placed too near the edge of the table.

"I ain't shittin' you, man. This old broad is crazy, Leo. She's gonna feed us to the cats!" With wild-eyed panic, he held both hands to his throat as he began backing toward the door.

Leo gaped at his partner for an instant, and then jumped up to join him. "Look, lady, we gotta get goin' now. My friend is obviously trippin' out or something'. It was nice talkin' to you an' all, but, uh, time to go." He nodded his head slightly and followed Jackson toward the door.

The woman stood and moved with unexpected agility to stand between them and the door. "Are you sure you have to go so soon, boys? I can get you an aspirin or something. Maybe you'll feel better."

"Fuck that! We're outta here." Jackson shoved her hard and grabbed for the doorknob, turning it quickly and opening the door.

As they fled into the hallway, the woman tumbled to the floor. A large carving knife was knocked from her hand on impact and skidded to a stop a few feet away. Somehow, she had concealed her intention beneath the kitchen towel she was still clutching as she struggled to get up. Neither man hesitated long enough to realize they had made a narrow escape. They hurried to the stairs and rapidly made their way down.

"What was that shit about, man? Why'd you go all spooky on my ass?" Leo sounded irritated.

"That old bitch poisoned us or something with those cookies! We need to get our asses to the hospital before it kicks in!"

They hit the landing and Jackson rushed to open the door and stumbled down the steps to the sidewalk. Leo grabbed the back of his jacket and spun him around to face him. "You watch too many movies, man. Get your shit together," he yelled in his face.

"Tell me you feel normal right now. Tell me you aren't getting a cramp in your stomach right about now," Jackson screamed back at him and kept on moving toward the street.

"Uh, now that you…" Leo stopped as he bent over with severe pain in his gut. "Fuck me! Get to the truck!" Both men ran for the SUV, and Leo fumbled with the keys, dropping them in the gutter as he tried to locate the door lock remote.

"I can't feel my fingers," he yelled as he tried to scoop up the key ring. When at last he was able to get his fingers around it, he hit the button. The door locks clicked and they both jumped in. Leo turned the key and the truck roared to life as he pushed the pedal to the floor. His legs were feeling heavy causing him to press harder than was necessary. The men lurched in their seats as the SUV was thrown into drive and the truck shot down the street.

"I think I just pissed myself," moaned Jackson.

"Whatta fuck's happenin?" Leo was slurring his words as he fell forward against the steering wheel.

Smaakrunch! The truck slammed into a metal street light pole. With the tinkling sound of glass falling to the sidewalk, Jackson was ejected from his seat straight through the windshield. The severed pole teetered for a moment and fell across the cab of the truck crushing Leo beneath it.

Twelve

The expressions on their faces were like children who had just walked into the most incredible toy store. The large, brightly lit armory was a bona fide, honest-to-God weapons depot. Each section was marked with a sign, and the aisles were organized by weaponry type. This would certainly facilitate a quick selection in case of an emergency. Frank stood near the door and watched the group wander through the aisles.

Emily was reading the signs aloud as she followed John. "Assault Rifles – Automatic, Semiautomatic, Bolt Action. Handguns – American, German, Hungarian, Czech. I didn't know there were so many kinds."

She continued, "Grenades, Mortars, Remote Detonation, C-4. Man, I think most people have never seen anything like this, let alone have it in their basement." She lowered her voice, "Is this legal?"

Across the room, they could hear a man's voice pick up where Emily left off. "Landmines, Field Artillery, Swords, Shields, Chain Mail? You got fuckin' chain mail in here, Frank?" It was Charles.

"I like to have a little bit of everything. Have you guys seen the phasers, tasers and lasers yet?"

"Over here." Max sounded a long way off.

Frank pulled a small device from his pocket, put it to his mouth and spoke. "Okay guys. Come back to the entrance door so we can talk about supplies." Frank's voice filled the room so there was no need to raise his voice.

Most of the group was back to the door in less than a minute, but Joe and Paulie were straggling. They moved slowly, touching the occasional weapon before joining the group. There was a look of total bliss on their faces.

"Is all this stuff real?" Emily asked somewhat timidly. She did not want to appear ignorant. Everyone else seemed so knowledgeable.

Frank laughed, "Not everything. Some are props from the games, mockups of weapons. I let the graphic designers play with them when we're developing a new series."

"You mean this shit's all toys?" Paulie looked disappointed.

"No, of course not!" Frank replied. "Most of the conventional hardware is real. The medieval stuff? Well, you could certainly kill someone with the swords, daggers, and crossbows, so I guess you could say they were real, but the phasers and other sci-fi shit? May as well be toys, but they're top notch replicas."

Phillip was eyeing one of the assault weapons on the rack to his left. "Looks like the game business has been really good to you, Frank."

"You'd be surprised how much money people are willing to spend pretending to kill people and break things. Five award winning games later, and here we are."

Frank turned to address all of them. "What good is it to have nice toys though if you can't play with somebody? Tell you what boys, uh, and... girl, grab any weapon you want, forty-five caliber and under. There are boxes of ammo on the shelves below each one. When you're ready, I have another surprise."

The guys ran for the shelves like shoppers at an 80% off sale on Black Friday. John was tempering his excitement. He felt like running with the rest of them, but was aware that Emily was studying his response. Instead of simply grabbing a gun for himself, he turned to Emily. "So tell me, wild thing, ever fired a gun before?"

"Well, when I was about twelve or thirteen, my father used to take me with him up in the foothills to shoot cans, but that was a long time ago." She didn't seem too thrilled, but then she smiled, "I'll take a 9mm Smith and Wesson M&P if ya got one, please."

John was amazed. All he could think was *what else don't I know about this girl?* He scanned the signs along the wall. As he approached the shelves, he could see the 9mm pistols, then the S&W logo.

Emily followed him, "Great, honey, I can get this from here. Go get yourself something cute to play with. I'll meet you at the door."

"Cute!" John couldn't help but chuckle at that one.

Thirteen

Just when the crew thought it could not get any better, surprise! Frank took them farther down the hall to another door. Inside was a lobby area decorated with several cocktail tables and plush furniture. It resembled an upscale modern lounge at first glance. There was a fully stocked bar and an old fashioned jukebox that had been modified to play from a selection of over a million songs of all types of music.

Beautifully framed signs hung on either side of the lobby proclaiming, "Please wear eye and ear protection." Between the doors was another sign on the wall that cheerfully read, "Enjoy Your Mission."

"I can't even imagine what we're gonna find in there." Max grinned with anticipation and a look of wonder on his face. "Frank?"

"Lady and gentlemen, if you could have anything you wanted to complement a full armory, what would it be?" Frank was beginning to sound like a ringmaster at a circus beckoning the audience to see the woman with the devil's tail.

Joe was quick to answer, "That women would find me irresistible!" He grinned.

"*That's* not gonna happen!" Emily said. Everyone laughed.

"Step right this way!" Frank waved his arm and walked toward the door to the left. Opening it, he moved inside.

As they entered into the room, the lights came on and a female voice cooed at them from hidden speakers saying, "Good day. Be sure to wear your eye and ear protection," before declaring more forcefully, "The shit is about to hit the fan!"

If Emily had closed her eyes, she might have thought she was in the middle of a crowd at a July fireworks display. The *oohs* and *ahs* that were coming from the group revealed just how impressed they were. It was the most incredible shooting range any had ever seen. There were ten lanes, one for each of them, and each was stocked with goggles, ear protection, targets and anything else that could be required.

The setup was high tech with bright LED lighting and range meters that told you the exact distance to the target. Wind simulators could generate velocities at up to fifty miles per hour to simulate any condition, and there was a separate control panel for each lane. There was built-in noise cancellation technology to reduce the sound of the firing weapons.

"Okay guys, get some practice. We want to be ready for what's ahead." Frank walked toward his lane with John following a few feet before asking, "What's ahead?"

"You know what's ahead, John. Step Three…" Frank waited for him to fill in the blank.

They both said it at once, "Ambush!"

Fourteen

The week following the meeting at Frank's house saw each member of the team coming and going as plans were laid out for every detail of the operation that was before them. The mob that was searching for Emily had to be exterminated like the cockroaches they were. The time was at hand.

Early in the morning under the cover of darkness on the eighth day, Archer and Joe were dispatched. Using customized igniters and traditional accelerants, they successfully destroyed both nightclubs that made up the center of operation for the gang's prostitution and drug distribution businesses.

When that was accomplished, several shady individuals who had been hired by friends of Frank's attorneys hit the street with a compelling story to spread inside the criminal community. In combination with selected friends of a few of the team members, these individuals were tasked to get the chatter bouncing off the brick-walled alleys around the city's streets. It was a message of all out aggression from a rival gang of mobsters. It would be impossible to ignore.

There was a certain amount of faith in the well-known methods of gangsters. John's friends were very sure they had enraged the bosses of their enemies enough to draw them out. The success of the operation depended on stereotypical behaviors and they were hopeful that they had made the right call. As far as they could tell, all the signs and feedback in the community pointed to success.

The plan for the evening was to meet at a nice restaurant for an early dinner. After that, they would head over to the warehouse that Frank had secretly purchased several days before. His attorney had tweaked the paperwork to give the appearance that he represented the owners of the nightclubs. They meticulously manipulated the process, assuring Frank that the transaction could never be traced.

The armaments and explosives were loaded and driven to the location during the previous night. Max and Philip had spent the past forty-eight hours preparing the building. They installed wiring for surveillance cameras and sensors. There was no way that any activity could go undetected. Special doors were built and hung in place. Every possible avenue of entry or exit had been fortified. Although it was a massive undertaking, the building was ready on schedule.

At 6 p.m. exactly, Frank, John and Emily pulled into the parking lot of the upscale diner. They got out of the car, all three dressed in black and wearing dark sunglasses. Several people stopped and stared as they walked up to the door. Once inside, they went directly to the very large booth in the back. The others were there ahead of them and had already ordered soft drinks and coffee.

"Hey guys." John greeted them. He couldn't help but notice that Joe was the only one not wearing black. "What's shakin?"

Clark was the first to respond. "Nothin' yet, but it's gonna be quakin' soon's we get this rat hunt started!"

A quiet "oorah" came from the group, and Emily looked around to see if anyone had noticed as they slid into the booth.

"Everything ready?" Frank was looking at Max who was nodding enthusiastically.

"Oh yeah," confirmed Philip. "We mapped the ordinance and marked every location with radioactive paint so you can see it with night vision." He grinned. "It'll shine, but the bad guys won't see shit."

"Perfect, and the light timers are set?" John asked.

"Sure thing, John Boy! When we cut the power to the main lights, you'll have ten clicks to get down the hall to the kill room." Max was grinning. "That is if your lazy ass can run that fast."

He looked at Frank. "Think you can do it, boss? Or should we reset that to twenty?"

"Smart ass!" Frank pulled his arm back as if he was going to slap him, and then smiled.

Emily had been watching this group of men interact for nearly two weeks. She never failed to marvel at their camaraderie and their ability to function so easily as a team. Frank definitely had charge of the group, but she believed it was mostly due to the fact that he was providing the resources for this operation. She wasn't exactly thrilled with the way they planned to deal with her situation, but in her heart, she believed there was no alternative.

"Guys," she started, "I'd like to tell you something I've been thinking for the past week." She spoke rather softly so they leaned closer to hear better. Ten men, each lethal in their own right, possibly killers, probably heroes, and she had their full attention.

"I know that what you are about to do tonight is no small thing. There is no way to know how many scumbags you will be dealing with, or how well armed they may turn out to be. Whatever happens, I want you all to know that never in my life, before John that is…"

She paused for a second, turning her head to look at him before continuing, "Never has anyone ever stepped up to help me when I was in trouble, especially bad shit like this, and now I am here with not just one, but ten heroes willing to step up and risk their lives to keep me safe."

Her eyes began to tear up, droplets inching down her cheeks. "I wanted to tell you all, every one of you, how much I appreciate you and will forever be indebted to you for the sacrifices you are willing to make for someone you hardly know. I will never be able to thank you enough. Still, I wanted to say it. Thank you."

It seemed everything in the diner had come to a halt, and for her, it was almost as uncomfortable as for the men sitting facing her. As if on cue, Joe broke the silence. "Ain't nothing but a thang, ma'am." His grin spoke volumes.

It was enough to snap the others out of their zoned out expressions. Another simultaneous "oorah" echoed through the sparsely filled dining area.

"Okay, let's try not to attract too much attention." John was not smiling as he looked around the room. "We need to stay incognito for now."

Frank looked at him and laughed saying, "Yeah, as incognito as nine dudes all dressed in black, plus one fashion outcast can be." He tipped his head toward Joe continuing, "All piled into a giant booth with one damned good looking woman."

John laughed, "You've got a point, buddy. She's like a diamond sittin' in a pile of gravel."

Fifteen

They arrived at the warehouse in a black SUV under the cover of darkness. Emily was driving, her hands gripped tightly on the wheel as she pulled into the parking lot and took the space nearest the door. Like a choreographed routine, two identical vehicles followed suit, parking on either side.

John looked at her from the passenger seat as Emily turned off the lights and sat with her foot on the brake. "Now remember, go straight to the house, no stops. Before you pull into the drive, make sure nobody is follow…" She was giving him *the look*. "… uh, but you know all that, right?" The concern he felt for her was plowing deep furrows across his forehead.

"Yes." She was looking at him, through him and into the very center of his being. "John, you know you guys didn't have to do this. I mean, if anything happens to you or one of the guys, I'll never forgive my…"

He pressed his gloved finger against her lips. "I… we had to do this. For the first time in my life, I can say this." He took a deep breath, cleared his throat, and continued, "I love you. More than I ever, in any relationship, with any other woman, I mean…"

John was struggling with the words. "If not taking care of this meant I had to live without you, well, it wouldn't be worth living."

Without a word, she unfastened her seatbelt as he spoke and threw herself across the column that separated them. Wrapping her arms around him, she covered his mouth with hers. He kissed her long and hard, and she returned his passion. He felt a rush as his libido kicked in, and he drank her in, holding her tightly to him until…

"Come on, people!" From the back seat, Frank broke in. "You can get a room later!"

John put his hands up to gently tip her head forward and kissed her again, this time on her forehead. "Drive carefully, and don't worry about us. We got this. By tomorrow we'll be free to do whatever we want."

He smiled reassuringly and opened the door to step out onto the pavement. Pressing the button to lock the door, he closed it and walked away toward the warehouse with Frank. By then, the rest of the team had vacated their trucks and were now waiting inside.

The sun was low in the sky behind her, and from across town darkness was racing toward them. As the two men headed to the door and slipped inside, Emily looked at herself in the mirror. Wiping the tears from her face, she backed out of the parking space. She was on her way back to Frank's house and safe haven, but she feared for John and his friends. Though she was grateful for her own safety, it was no comfort.

In the warehouse, the men were preparing for the battle ahead. They buckled on their utility belts loaded with stun and smoke grenades, extra ammo, and hefty fighting knives in case things got close. John and Frank pulled their shirts off over their heads and helped each other fasten the straps as they put on their body armor. Slipping their shirts back on, they joined the rest to weapon up.

"This reminds me of that scene from Rambo where Stallone is putting on his shit before going to kill a bunch of motherfuckers." Joe laughed and pretended to tie on a bandana with obvious glee. "I wish I had a fuckin' bandana to tie around my head." It seemed he was looking forward to the kill.

"You could wear your red underwear on you head, you crazy bitch," joked Paulie. "It's all good once you get past the skid marks!"

"Yeah, if I *was* wearing underwear, and you oughta know about skid marks, ya nasty fuck," Joe fired back.

They sniped back and forth for a few minutes longer, mostly ignored by the rest of the team. It was their way of getting juiced up for the mission ahead. John had seen it many times in Iraq. Finally, a hush fell over the room. All that could be heard was the sound of the last few straps being fastened and magazines being slapped into weapon chambers.

When Frank and John had verified that all weapons were loaded and everything was ready at the predetermined locations, John loudly cleared his throat and began to speak. "I can't tell you this is gonna be easy, or that we're all gonna walk outta here of our own accord when this shit is over."

He rubbed his chin and looked at the men as he spoke. "What I can say is that this act of friendship, of loyalty, will not be forgotten by Emily or myself. We will forever be indebted to your willing sacrifice here tonight. As long as I live, I will always have your backs wherever, whenever."

John paused to compose himself. "And when we walk out of this..."

"Geezus!" Frank interrupted, "John, you don't have to thank us, man. We're just here for the beer, right, marines?"

"Sir, yes sir!" came the chorused reply.

"Gentlemen, take your positions, and don't forget your goggles." Frank smiled at John, bowed and waved his arm. "After you."

Sixteen

Joe had been relieved from direct combat duty due to the burn injury he had sustained while taking out the nightclubs. From his position on the roof of the warehouse, his role in this operation was to notify the team when the mob arrived. When the action started, he would make sure that not one of their targets escaped alive.

Frank had estimated that there might be about fifteen to twenty mobsters, but in the distance, Joe could see a caravan of ten or twelve black SUVs traveling without headlights. There could be no doubt who was coming, but how many were there?

"Anybody got a guess how many assholes fit into an Escalade?" There was an audible click as his mike cut off.

"Four, maybe five if they're all puckered up in the back seat. Whatcha got up there, Joe?" John glanced over at Frank.

"I got about ten or twelve of 'em pulling in right now, but I can't get a look inside. The windows are tinted."

"It is what it is, Joe. Let 'em get inside the building, but don't let 'em get out. You got that?" Frank responded into his mike.

"Yes sir, the party is on. Good hunting. Joe out."

He crouched down below the edge of the building and watched on his handheld screen the feed from the cameras that had been mounted on the outside of the building. There was some commotion as the trucks unloaded and the crew split into two groups. One went for the front door while the other was waved around to the back. From what he could see on his screen, it looked like they had plenty of firepower and there had to be at least sixty or more thugs working their way toward the doors.

"I got about sixty or more, you getting the feed? They're loaded for bear."

"We hear you Joe. Don't let the roaches scatter. Everybody get that?" John spoke into his headset and adjusted the night vision goggles that had been resting atop his head. A round of "ayes" echoed in his earpiece.

Just then, he heard the outside door open. There were footsteps coming from the dimly lit hallway. It had been specially constructed from thin drywall and two-by-fours spaced farther apart than usual. Built to double back on itself like the caged lines of an amusement park ride, the aim was to allow a very large group to enter the building before the guys in the lead could see anything in the room where John and Frank were waiting.

It was a good thing that the hall was wide because at least thirty guys were pouring in through the door. Another thirty or more were headed around the sides to the rear of the building. This was a very old building and there were only two doors through which to enter, aside from the rolling doors of the loading dock. Both of them had been left unlocked and, within minutes, everyone had moved inside. To Joe, it was like watching ants marching into a hole in the ground.

The men who entered through the front of the building were the most dangerous looking of the group. They were carrying assault rifles and shotguns, all of them at the ready. Some sent red pinpoints from laser sights bouncing off the walls as they walked down the hall. Following behind some of the biggest guys were two gang leaders, bosses of the entire San Francisco and Oakland operations. Joe figured they believed a couple of bodyguards could protect them from the hellacious slaughter that was about to take place.

As the gangsters rounded the final turn into the room, they could see John and Frank sitting on opposite sides of a long table positioned beneath a single shaded light bulb. A slight haze of dust was giving substance to its glow. There was just enough light emitting from the bulb to reveal the faces of the two men sitting there, while dark shadows concealed the night vision goggles resting atop their heads.

Pushing past the thugs standing before him, one of the bosses yelled across the room, "Are you the motherfuckers that burned down our clubs?" He had not been holding a gun when he asked the question, but reached behind his back, produced one and began waving it around.

John could hear Joe in his earpiece. "All inside, front and back."

"You talking to us?" John yelled back, mustering up his best voice of surprise.

"You assholes have fucked with the wrong per…"

The words had barely escaped his lips before the boss noticed John and Frank reaching for something. He craned his neck, straining to see what it could be. The men at the table pulled their night vision goggles into position. Almost in the same instant, the last of the gang who had just entered the building heard the solid clunk of the double bolts that slid into place and securely locked the heavy steel door behind them.

Now they realized something was wrong. As they ran back to push against the door, all of the lights in the building went out leaving them in complete darkness. Frank put his hands on the tabletop and vaulted over it to land next to John. As Frank's feet hit the ground, he slammed his palm down on a large button attached to the tabletop.

"Let's party!" he yelled as the two front legs of the table folded in. The heavily armored table dropped in an arc onto its side, slamming into the concrete floor to form a large shield in front of them.

The mobster shouted into the darkness at the group of thugs trying to find their targets with the red lasers. "What are you waiting for, assholes? Shoot!"

Automatic weapon fire lit up the room. John and Frank had dropped to the floor behind the table. Sliding panels allowed them to open gun ports at any level. They began low, spraying lead in both directions ahead of them several inches from the floor. Their state of the art Kalashnikovs fired hundreds of rounds per minute in dampened bursts.

Bullets cut through the thin sheetrock and hit panic crazed men standing in the blackness of the hallway. There were screams of agony as armor piercing bullets ripped muscle and flesh from their legs. Bones were shattered and return fire rang out. The mobsters' bullets ricocheted off the hard metal and concrete walls causing even more hazards for the attackers.

Frank pulled a handle behind the tabletop and another panel shot out to create a tall shield between the two men and the gunfire that was lighting up the other side of the room. The sound of weapons firing and lead hitting the metal table was deafening. The voice in their earpieces was counting down and John could barely hear it well enough to count along in his head, six, five, four...

A loud explosion came from the front entrance followed by screams as the thugs who had been trying to escape were shattered by shrapnel. John and Frank ran for the door to the large center of the warehouse. This was the kill room and the gunfire continued behind them as they hit the door and headed through it.

Frank yelled into his microphone, "Go!"

***

At the rear of the building, the rest of the thugs were trapped in a large windowless room with two doors. The steel door where they had entered was reinforced and, no matter what they tried, it would not open. The door ahead of them seemed highly reinforced as well. Two men held up butane lighters and looked around for a way out. They could hear the mayhem coming from the front of the building, but there was no way to get out of the room to help.

The sounds of automatic weapons and death screams caused the trapped men to become agitated, and they began to work themselves into a fit of frenzy like hornets in a nest that had been shaken. As cigarette lighters flicked on and off, the chorus of chaos began to rise. Loud shouts of anger and frustration reflected their level of panic.

"How the fuck do we get outta here?"

"I dunno. The fuckin' doors are locked tight!"

"Break the fuckers down!"

"We tried."

"What the hell? Let's go!"

***

"2, 1..." John finished the countdown as the door closed behind him and all the lights in the room they had just vacated came on. The haze of gun smoke made any view of the carnage difficult in the dim light. The table was lying on its side, the gleaming surface riddled with dents from the impact of high caliber slugs. The makeshift wall of the hallway had fallen over, apparently cut down from the impact of gunshots and the thugs slamming into it as they tried to escape.

Half the men were either lying on the floor moaning or were scattered about in bits of gore near the locked exterior door. The door itself had marks on it from the blast but stood like a monument of death before them. One of the gang leaders had been torn apart by gunfire and lay in a shredded heap on the concrete. The other had taken a shot to his shoulder and stood glaring silently at what was left of his crew. His hand over the wound, he applied pressure in an attempt to stop the blood that was pouring from the jagged bullet hole.

"What the hell are you waiting for?" he yelled at the only men left standing there with him. "Get those motherfuckers!"

"But, Boss…" One of the bodyguards whose leg had been nearly shot off, struggled to remain on his feet. He was bleeding out in a puddle around his one good foot.

"You got a fucking problem?" The boss yelled, aiming his pistol at the man's head. He squeezed the trigger and planted a slug in his brain.

"Anybody else got a problem?" he shrieked, his voice cracking. "Shoot those motherfuckers dead, right now! GO!" It was obvious that he had lost any capacity for rational thought.

Anyone who was able, moved toward the door at the other end of the room. The boss followed, seeking cover behind the human shield in front of him. There were only about ten or twelve men in all. The man in front warily grabbed the doorknob, opened the door and stepped quickly to the side to avoid any gunfire. There was nothing, no resistance at all, so they filed cautiously into the room.

Through the doorway was a large open warehouse full of boxes stacked as high as eight feet. There was open passage to the left and to the right, which was clear in both directions. As the men walked out into the center of the warehouse, several explosions came from behind them in the room they had just vacated. Anyone straggling behind now scrambled for the door. Finally, the door was closed leaving behind those who were still trying to crawl toward it.

***

At the rear of the building, the men trapped there had given up trying to escape to the street. Some sat on the floor, while others worked at opening the interior door. At last, it clicked to release the lock.

One man celebrated and slapped the back of the one who had managed to unlock the door. "Hell yeah, Louie!"

"I didn't do anything, man. I wasn't touchin' it."

Louie began to back away while another man nearer to the door pushed it open to reveal a large room filled with stacks of boxes. Moving as one unit, the group slowly and cautiously shuffled in, hoping to find an exit somewhere else in the building.

Two men at the back of the group spoke quietly, wondering whether they might have walked into another trap. It was obvious there was no other way out, so they went on through the door with the rest of the group. Suddenly, both doors at each end of the room locked behind them, the bolts sliding back into place with barely a sound as they sealed the thugs in the center of the large warehouse.

The men split up taking their orders now from a couple of bigger guys who had taken charge. Some went to the left and some to the right. They cautiously wound their way through the maze of boxes, carefully clearing each corner before moving forward.

John and Frank led their crew stealthily through an exit that led up to the roof. They sealed the door behind them and ran to the edge. One by one, they climbed down the emergency ladder that hung from the side of the building.

Joe was waiting at ground level. He helped them with their weapons as they stepped and jumped the final few feet to the ground. As the last man landed firmly on the pavement, the team was already moving to the front of the building. Philip pulled a small remote from his pocket, flipped a clear plastic safety cover open, and pressed the red button.

***

Inside the cavernous warehouse, the silence was deafening as the men weaved between the rows in the darkness. Each one attempted to avoid bumping into anything that might draw attention to the group. Unfortunately, one of the guys who had suffered severe wounds to his leg in the ambush stumbled and fell against a stack of boxes, knocking it over.

"What the fuck! Them boxes is empty," one of the thugs blurted. With that, he kicked over another stack.

"What's that smell?" asked another.

"Shit! That's the stuff we use to make meth!"

"Holy mother! We gotta get out of here now," yelled someone.

"Whad you say?"

"It's ether, man!"

***

Piling into their vehicles, the team made their escape maneuvering easily past the cars that had been parked behind them. John was relieved that they had not been blocked in. Now that they were more than a block away, he watched, as the building grew smaller in the rearview mirror.

"You're sure they can't get out of there?" he asked the man behind the wheel. Charles was intent on putting some distance between them and the warehouse.

In the back seat, Max was holding a second small remote in his hand. "They aren't goin' nowhere. We got double titanium bolt locks on those doors and right about now the ether should be kickin' their asses."

"Damn, where'd you get ether? That's what was in those drums?"

"You don't want to know. I think it's time for some fireworks." Flipping the switch on the device in his hand to activate the pulsing red light, Max pushed the button.

***

In the room at the center of the warehouse, the men were coughing as fumes filled the room. They were beginning to lose consciousness unaware of the device hanging from the rafters above their heads. When the arc of electricity sparked between its contacts, rolling flames instantly filled the building. It was a blast furnace of epic proportions, perhaps offering any man yet conscious a flash preview of their final destination.

The shockwave jolted the team from behind as a boiling sea of flames engulfed the streets surrounding the warehouse and shot into the night sky.

Seventeen

Emily got a glimpse of the headlights as the trucks pulled into the driveway of Frank's sprawling home. White-knuckled, she had a tight grip on the magazine she had been reading to occupy herself. Standing now, she tossed it back to the table. She was eager to confirm that John was alive and well, and ran to greet the men.

She stood at the front door watching through the sidelight windows until the vehicles came to a stop, then she opened the door and stepped out onto the front steps with her arms crossed over her breasts. She was relieved to see that both trucks appeared to be full of passengers.

At last, the men came spilling out of the trucks and Emily slowly exhaled, as her feet started moving. She felt the tears welling in her eyes as she ran to John and threw her arms around him. "Thank God you're all right," she whispered, breathless and husky. She hugged him again more tightly. "I don't know what I would... if..."

"Shhh, it's okay," he stopped her. "It's all over now." He held on to her tightly. He loved the feel of her arms around him, and his body tingled at her touch. He was learning to relax and enjoy being with her without over thinking it. It felt like home.

Frank stood back from the group eyeing the men. It appeared that there were no injuries. "Let's go inside, people. We need to debrief."

The group fell in line and headed inside, all but Emily and John. Still wrapped in each other's arms, Frank gave John's shoulder a pat as he walked past them. At that, the lovers peeled themselves apart and followed Frank up the walkway.

The men paused in the large entry room, and Paulie was the first to break the silence just as the couple joined them. "I feel kinda bad in a way." He took his hat off and scratched his head. "I know they were bad guys and everything, but what a shitty way to go."

"Get over it, Paulie," Clark had kept to himself during the ride back to the house, but it was not over some kind of guilty conscience. "Did you think we could bring 'em flowers, ask for a favor, and everything would be all right?"

"Man, I know what you're sayin' but, damn, I can't stop thinking bout them bein' trapped in that room and shit. I know I don't wanna go out that way myself. I fuckin' hate fire!" Paulie wiped the palms of his hands on his t-shirt.

Frank had just walked in. "You guys get cleaned up, okay? We can talk about this over a couple shots of single malt. I have a bottle that I've been saving for a special occasion. Meet you back in the great room when you're ready, and we'll get some perspective on all of this."

The guys headed up the stairs that led to the guest rooms, leaving John and Emily standing there with Frank. "We did the right thing," offered Frank, "and no one should have any doubts."

"I know it better than anyone." John looked him straight in the eyes. "Those guys were as bad as any terrorists, if not worse. What we did today, although distasteful, well, we saved the lives of a lot of innocent people. This town is safer tonight because of what we did."

Emily put her arm around John. "What you guys did tonight, you didn't just save my life. You saved me from a living hell. They were coming for me, and I would have never been able to live without fear. God knows how many others they were after."

"Well, if anyone is having second thoughts, I'm sure they'll get over it quick enough." Frank turned as a voice came from the stairway behind him.

"Who's got a problem?" It was Joe. "Ain't nobody got a problem with that shit. We took out lotsa bad guys tonight, same as Iraq. Take out the bad guys so the good folks can be free and happy. Send No Angel, right, John?"

Emily gave John a puzzled look, "What does that mean?"

"When we were in Iraq, they used to say that before every mission. Send No Angel, to do the Devil's work." He nodded over at Joe. "You got it, buddy, Send No Angel."

Emily put her arm around John's waist. "Send No Angel. That's some statement to make."

"In the middle of a battle, it's them or you. I can't think of anything that carries more meaning, or more effectively defines the job that has to be done."

"I'm sorry you had to go through…"

John cut her off before she could finish. "It's a part of who I am now. It made me a better person." He pulled her tight against him as though nothing or no one could ever come between them.

If only life could be like that.

Eighteen

Several days after the warehouse fire, Emily finally persuaded John to make some anonymous calls to authorities concerning the aliens they had left behind in the NorthWest forest. He had resisted the idea at first, wanting to avoid getting involved in any major investigation, but Emily couldn't sleep well until it was reported. She needed to put the incident behind her and have some assurance that the monsters would not survive to kill anyone else.

They planned to use public phones at different locations to make three calls. First, they would contact the local authorities, and then the forestry service. The last call would be made to the FBI. John rehearsed the story repeatedly as they drove around town searching for a public phone. These days, pay phones were hard to find.

First stop, the bus station. To prevent anyone getting their tag number, he backed into a parking space against the building cautious to watch for any surveillance cameras. Using the phone card that Emily had purchased with cash, John wore cotton gloves to make the call. He timed the call to prevent any trace. Rinse, repeat. They moved on to find the next phone.

They were able to locate another phone at a homeless shelter. Emily was pleased that she had thought of it. Of course, it would be the down-on-their-luck types who would still require a pay phone. Then John got the idea to try the historic area a few miles away. He was glad to find the red pay phone stall still there in the old drugstore. It was an antique, but it still worked.

All three agencies seemed interested in the information John provided, asking as many questions as they could get in before John ended the calls.

Days went by and Emily became obsessed with checking the news, poring over all the local reports she could find. If she wasn't watching the news, she was surfing the internet, sometimes using her touch-screen tablet to do both at the same time. Finally, she found what she was looking for. A website dedicated to so-called government leaks posted, "An unidentified source has reported that alien life forms wreaking havoc in Umatilla National Forest are the target of an ongoing effort by the U.S. military. Their mission is to exterminate the creatures. It is believed the aliens may be responsible for several missing persons in the area."

Emily felt her heartbeat in her throat as she continued to read. "Recent wildfires in the area were likely engineered as cover for the top secret operation." The article ended with the usual disclaimer, "The information in this report has not been confirmed."

Somehow, reading the report helped to relieve Emily's survivor guilt. At least she no longer felt the need to talk about it ten times a day. John hoped she would soon begin to forget about what had happened at the warehouse so they could get back to living their life without regrets. Fortunately, she had not seen that carnage up close and personal. She would not have to relive the images of death every time she closed her eyes.

Nineteen

The chill breeze rolling down the mountains from the east was proof that winter was fast approaching. John and Emily had rented a small apartment in an older home in the heart of San Francisco and were looking forward to building their life together. Emily's cat had found his new home to be more than adequate, staking his claim in the front room where the afternoon sun warmed the small rug she had used to protect the back of John's arm chair. Ralph spent most of his days curled up there, occasionally gazing out the window at anything that moved.

Frank and the other men had returned to their lives, frequently communicating by email and text messages. It meant a lot to John that he could stay in touch with the other men. He would forever be in their debt for what they had done to help him eliminate the threat to Emily's life. He knew in his heart that if any of them ever needed his help, he would be there for them without hesitation, no matter what.

In the days following the warehouse incident, an investigation had been conducted by local law enforcement. The police concluded that there had been a meth lab accident in the vacant warehouse. According to them, a catastrophic explosion and the resulting fire had consumed a major northern California criminal organization. Although news reports reflected some skepticism that what happened was an accident, the media in general seemed to consider it a blessing. In the words of one local reporter, "*Citizens of the Bay Area can sleep more soundly tonight knowing that the streets of the city are safer.*"

Requests for further investigations had been rejected by the district attorney who was the recipient of large campaign contributions from one generous supporter, Franklin DeMint. Big gun lawyers hired by the families of gang members pushed legal requests through every branch of the courts only to find that local officials balked at reopening the case, deeming it unwarranted. In fact, officials in both local and federal law enforcement agencies were able to close the books on hundreds of cases.

John sat in his office staring at the phone. He picked it up and listened for a dial tone to make sure it was actually working. He sighed and shook his head wondering why they had invested in an old-school landline phone service. Emily had insisted that they keep their business and personal lives separated, and he refused to carry two phones in his pocket.

She had made a good case for going home at the end of the day without the interruption of business calls during their evenings together and extolled the tax advantages of keeping their expenses separated. He had to admit, there was a lot they could write off, including the oversized office space, but now he was stuck with a large wooden desk and a clunky old phone.

Their new paranormal investigation business was off to a slow start. This afternoon the sun striped the room with long shadows from the window blinds, and John was starting to drift off to sleep. When the phone rang, he nearly jumped out of his chair. *Had Emily turned up the volume on the ringer, or was it actually that quiet in here today?* Maybe it was a combination of the two. He let it ring a couple of times to give the caller the impression of a busy office.

On the third ring, he answered, "Hazard and Sparks Investigations, Hazard speaking. How can we help you today?" He had put on his most professional voice.

"John, it's me," Emily said on the other end of the line. "That sounded really good, hon. Very professional."

"Thanks," he sat back again, somewhat disappointed. "I've been practicing. What are you up to?"

"I just left the house, you know the one we talked about, my appointment today?"

"Yes."

"Well, it went really well. In fact, we start the job next week. But, honey, the best part is, when they asked how much, I was so excited I just blurted out five thousand plus expenses."

"Holy shit!" Now she had his attention. "And they said yes?"

"Yep. We set up next Wednesday. John, it's a huge, beautiful old house, sits on top of this hill, and…"

"Tell me again what the problem is there?" He cringed as the words left his mouth. He was trying to learn not to cut people off when they spoke. It was part of Emily's "be the best we can be" program, though he had begun to believe it was a program designed specifically for him. She was so excited that she didn't call him on it.

"Well, actually it's more than one issue. If I had to guess, I'd say it was poltergeists, but this place is crazy, John. I think I saw ghosts while I was there. Cat ghosts."

"Cats? As in Ralph-type cats?"

"Well, not exactly like Ralph. They seemed bigger, and their fur was matted. Well, it wasn't just the fur really… um…" She searched for words to describe what she saw. "I

don't know how to say this, but it was like they wanted…
to eat me."

"You could actually see them?"

"Not quite, I mean, when I was talking to the owner, I
kept seeing some kind of movement. You know, out the
corner of my eye, like right beside me."

"You think they wanted to eat you? What made you
think…"

"It's just a feeling, John. I don't know, call it a
woman's intuition, but when you have a ghost cat sitting on
an end table next to you, glaring at you with huge red eyes,
licking his chops, I don't think it means it wants to be
petted. Do you?"

"Sounds like that house has some history. Those are
pretty strong apparitions for daylight."

"John, I'm telling you. I could have sworn it was right
there next to me, and when I tried to look directly at it,
there was nothing there. But, there's more."

"Don't tell me there were monster hamsters, too,
'cause I'm not too fond of…"

"Oh, you're hilarious." He could hear the aggravation
in her voice. "Look, whatever's in that house, it's a hell of a
lot less dangerous than those fuckin' aliens you introduced
to me."

He knew better than to try to interject any more
humor. He did not want to start something. In the more
than six months they had been together, he had yet to win
an argument, especially when it involved the NorthWest
trip. "Yeah, you're probably right. I don't think ghost cats
can be all that scary."

"Well, the one on the end table that was looking to eat
me was bad enough but, when the owner took me into the
kitchen, I got a good look at a ghost of a woman." There

was a long pause. "I've never seen anything like it in my worst nightmares, John, or even in any movies, especially something like that involving a woman."

"She wasn't having sex with that cat bastard, was she?"

"NO! Why do guys automatically go there? Geezus, John. There was a woman there, I mean, not really. You know what I mean. She had one of those big meat cleavers in her hand."

"What? She was butchering the cat?"

"Will you let me finish? No, she was NOT butchering the cat. She was hacking up some guy. Her victim probably didn't let *her* finish what she was trying to say." She coughed for emphasis. "The cats were eating the bits of him that were falling to the floor, lapping up the blood like they were drinking milk from a saucer."

"Okay... and you're excited about this gig?"

"Come on, John. We can't live off Frank's loan forever. Of course, I'm not excited about cannibal ghost cats. I'm excited about getting the job, aren't you? Well, I guess they weren't cannibals 'cause they weren't eating other cats…" Her thoughts had wandered. "Aagh! You know what I mean!"

"Okay, Em. Look, why don't you just head on home? I'll lock up here and meet you there."

"Yeah, want me to pick up something for dinner on my way?"

"What were you thinking? Sushi?" John knew she really loved sushi, but he had gotten sick on it once and felt queasy every time he tried eating it after that.

"No, I was thinking pizza. You know that place where they cook it on a grill?"

"I'm in. Get two. I think I can eat a whole one myself right now."

She hesitated before saying what she was thinking. "You know, honey, one of these days that's going to catch up with you. You aren't a teenager anymore."

"Yeah, tell that to my stomach!" He rubbed it, smiling.

He heard a sound as she ended the call without saying goodbye. It could be a difficult night. She only hung up like that when she was frustrated with him.

Twenty

Joe and Paulie sat at the bar, a near empty pitcher of beer between them. It was their third. "I keep meanin' to ask ya, Joe." Paul took a drink from his glass and wiped the foam from his lips before finishing his thought. "How's the leg?"

Joe opened his mouth to speak but, instead, issued a very loud extended belch. He formed the word, "Okay," as the burp came to its natural conclusion. He seemed very pleased with his achievement as he sported a glassy-eyed grin.

Nodding, he finally answered, "It's been healed up for a minute or two now. Got a good scar out of it though. Here, check it out."

He reached down and pulled up his pant leg revealing a wide scar on his calf. "Chicks dig scars, ya know." Letting his pant leg drop again, he grinned again. "I tell 'em I got it in Iraq. Now that's some magical shit, makes their clothes drop right off!"

"Speakin' of that shit, you think about it much?" Paulie took another swig.

"Gettin' laid?"

"No, I mean, I get these dreams, about Iraq, ya know?"

"Nah man, I don't dream. I just sleep and wake up. Ain't nuthin in between."

He hollered toward the bartender, "Can we get a menu? I'm fuckin' starving' over here!" Turning back to Paulie, he asked, "You hungry, man?"

"You know that's right. You buyin', are ya?"

"Oh yeah, I mean, NO!" Joe had bought lunch the last couple of times they had gotten together.

"I guess it's my turn then." Paulie pulled out his wallet and checked to see if he had any cash. Over his shoulder, Joe could see a couple of Franklins smiling out from the leather. "We good, bro."

They sat quiet for a moment, then Joe started, "About that shit in Iraq…" Looking sideways at Paulie, he lowered his voice and leaned toward his friend. "Ya think we should talk about that here?"

"I don't know, man. I been getting a weird feelin' lately, like something's gonna happen. Like I said, Joe, I been havin' dreams and shit, and Frank's involved somehow."

"Dreamin' about Frank? You ain't turning bitch on me are ya?" He reached out and gave Paulie a playful shove nearly knocking him from his seat.

"Hell no, I ain't turning bitch, bitch! For somebody who don't dream, you sure got some big imagination, ass-wipe." Paulie's face reddened a bit. Joe's joke about his sexuality had his hackles up, but he was not about to give him the pleasure of knowing he had gotten under his skin.

Joe leaned back and laughed. "Ya ain't gotta be a dreamer to worry bout your friends, bro." In a low tone, he added, "So what's in them dreams?"

"You serious? Now you wanna know, after talkin' all your smack? Hmph!" Paulie rubbed the whiskers around his jaw and started again, "I don't know what it means, but I saw Frank, and he was somewhere I never seen before, surrounded by these fuckin' things, ya know?"

He snarled and lifted his hands to give an indication of the size and intensity of the dream creature. "Frank was packin' iron and, geezus, he was shooting the shit out of 'em, but they just stood there soakin' up the lead and closin' right on in. I think he was askin' me for help. I woke up all sweaty and shit."

"Um, yeah, so it wasn't Iraq then?"

"Nah man, this was some other crazy ape shit place. Like it was daylight, but it wasn't. Bright enough, but there weren't no shadows."

"You mean like twilight, when the sun is just going down?" He waited for his friend to nod, but Paulie was just sitting there wide-eyed like a man who had seen a ghost. "Aw, man. What're you worryin' about? Sounds like you ate some bad chow before bed."

"Well, you might think that, except I been havin' that dream all the time lately."

"I know how you can make it stop. It works, and you don't gotta take pills."

"Yeah, what's that?"

"Don't go to sleep, man." He laughed loud and slapped Paulie on the back, yelling, "Hey! We gotta cook our own food or what? Can a starving war hero get a menu?" He turned to Paulie with one of his big goofy grins. "That war hero shit gets 'em every time."

Twenty-One

John and Emily sat eating their pizza. Neither spoke a word. Only the sound of John's chewing penetrated the silence as he gobbled down a few slices. He chased the cheesy bites with a cold beer while Emily sat watching him closely. She took her time slowly chewing each bite. She was still working on her first slice when she asked, "Are you mad at me?"

John finished swallowing his mouthful. "No, sexy, not at all. How about you? Mad at me?"

He recognized the risk he was taking to ask. He didn't know much about women, but he had learned it was better not to ask open-ended questions. Yet, he could see that something was troubling her. He could tell by the way that she held her head as she looked over at him. Opening the floodgates even a crack could be asking for trouble. Well, after sitting and waiting for the phone to ring all day in that dull lonely office, if she wanted to unload on him, game on. At least he would not be bored. There was always a chance for make up sex later.

"No, honey, I guess I'm just tired and a little bit frustrated."

Dare he ask? "What's frustrating, Em? You got that job for us today. You did good." He reached out across the table and took hold of her hand. "It's our first real job, you should feel good about it. Maybe we should be drinking champagne instead of beer?" He felt proud of himself for considering her feelings.

"Yeah, well you didn't sound too happy on the phone." She sighed deeply.

"Sure, I was happy." He wasn't too crazy about cats, truth-be-told. Somehow, he managed to tolerate Ralph for Emily's sake, but cannibal cat ghosts? How does that even happen? "Look, I know you've been working really hard to get us that first job. Starting a new business is tough, no matter what kind of business, and this job is something we can use to promote the services." He thought for a moment before adding, "This is a good thing for us." He knew it was true. Still, there were those damned cats.

"Well I hope you aren't just saying that to make me feel better. If so, well, thanks." She smiled at him. Her smile always melted his heart even in the middle of their most difficult times.

"No worries. I meant every word." Despite the fact that he dreaded even the thought of this particular job, somehow he managed to look her in the eyes. For cover, he took another bite of pizza.

Twenty-Two

Frank DeMint was back at his computer, the adrenalin coursing through his veins as he scrawled some notes on a scrap of paper. Had he actually done what he thought he had? The only way he could be sure was to do it again, but this time he was going to set the system timer for five minutes.

He was conducting his experiment in a specially constructed ground level computer lab furnished with some of the most sophisticated technology available, some still in the final stages of development and not yet available to the public. He was fortunate to be able to access such innovative equipment through his prestigious position in the gaming industry. Recently, he had received an extremely powerful multi-core processor that would render all others obsolete on the day that it hit the shelves.

He hoped his new setup would have the capacity to control The Machine, as he called it. No system he had assembled up to this point had the computing power necessary. The engineer who had helped him build his latest configuration of The Machine had doubted there was any processor in existence able to perform the calculations required to make it work. Finally, after three years of trial and error, the new processor could be the answer.

Plans for The Machine must have gone way back. Handwritten on scrolls made of some kind of animal skin, they appeared to be ancient. When he had worked through the scrawled instructions, and all the elements were finally assembled, the contraption was unlike any piece of equipment he had ever seen. Every part had been

manufactured by hand. Copper, brass, gold and silver had
been shipped to secret locations across the country where
individual parts were machined to extreme tolerances. Some
were beautifully intricate in their design, while others
appeared to be nothing but blocks drilled with complex
holes and tapped in order to attach the fittings.

The plans were followed to the letter as best as he
could figure. The finished apparatus was indeed a work of
art. Cryptic symbols were stamped into the outward surfaces
of many of its parts. Crowning the contraption was four 2-
inch round iron-reinforced copper rods, two of which stood
seven feet high, while the others were a couple of feet
shorter. Each rod was capped by a giant amethyst crystal,
seven inches by two and a half foot long. A delicate
framework of gold and silver held each gem in place. They
were set at various angles pointing toward a stone wall, a
seamless construct of sandstone.

Since his initial test, a scorch had remained on the
wall, no doubt a result of the intense energy that had been
focused there. It formed a rectangle beginning an inch from
the floor and spanning seven feet high and ten feet wide.
Frank recalled the moment the doorway, or some kind of
portal, had opened. The question was *a portal to where?*

He had recorded the entire experiment. A video
camera attached to a makeshift cart was pushed through the
portal just as the wall had opened up. He had intended only
to record for a few minutes, and then retrieve the rig using a
rope he had tied to the cart. However, a few seconds into it
he felt a tug on the rope. Disappointed, he was forced to
abort. Jerking the cart back through the hole, he found it
covered with scratches and some yellow dust but otherwise
free from major damage.

Although the recording revealed nothing but static,
one thing of note was the stench that filled the room when

the portal had opened. What had blown in from the other side was foul with a combination of rotting flesh and the odor that often overwhelms you in a porta-potty on a hot summer's day. *My god, what was over there?*

Frank dismantled the rig on the cart and put the camera back in the cabinet where he kept it. He carefully rolled the cart to the opposite side of the lab and covered it. He would clean it up later. He still had many unanswered questions, and planned to open the portal for another five minutes. He would step through it, get a quick look, and then immediately come back to the lab. He did not want to stay there for more than a minute. There was no way for him to know what he would encounter there, or how long the portal would remain open, so he felt it would be wise to keep it short.

A practical man, Frank had always been known for his well-considered plans, a habit that had served him well in Iraq and saved his team on many a mission. It made sense that he would plan this experiment around every possible scenario. On the desk beside him lay a 9mm pistol with a full magazine. He had put an extra clip in his pocket for good measure, though he did not expect to use it. He had made detailed notes on the nature of his research, what he planned to do, and how he was able to launch the apparatus to open the portal. His notes were carefully placed next to the computer just in case something went wrong.

Now he was ready to go. After typing his password, the machine began the initialization sequence. As he waited, he pulled his phone from his pocket and dialed John's number to leave a message. By the time he had finished, it was happening. The portal was opening. The machine began to emit a low hum as it vibrated, and then, a slight sizzling sound as the wall opened up before him.

Amazed at the technology he had assembled, Frank stood solemnly gathering his courage before taking a step into what he hoped would be an alternate world. As he moved toward the open passage, he remembered one important detail. He had not left the password. Without it, the system could not be initiated by someone else should it be necessary.

Turning back, he rushed to his desk. Quickly, he set the pistol down and grabbed a note pad and pen. After scratching out, "SEND_NO_ANGEL," he tore it off and stuck it on the large flat screen monitor. Taking a deep breath, he hastily jogged through the portal and disappeared leaving his gun behind.

Twenty-Three

Malcolm was working in near darkness beneath the overpass. He shook the can of green paint while he held the piece of cardboard against the concrete. The light that managed to find its way under the structure barely enabled him to see what he was doing, but he was used to the challenge. He thrived on surging adrenaline as he practiced the illicit art of graffiti.

The mural was beginning to take shape, and he figured he had about a half hour before someone saw him and reported him to the cops. He was painting clumps of tall grass in the scene when the phone in his pocket blared out his latest ringtone, electronic music with voice samples from "The Matrix." By the time he fished it from his pocket, he could hear Morpheus talking about the red pill.

"You got Mal," he said.

"Yeah, Mal. This is Phil…"

"Phil? What time is it, dude?"

"I think it's about 10:15 or so. The store's been closed for a while now."

"And you interrupted my latest masterpiece because?"

"You told me to call when those new big screens came in, remember? They're in, and you should see…"

Mal shook his spray can, the metal ball inside clacking while it mixed the paint. "Yeah, I remember. Can I come by when I'm done and throw one in the truck?"

"Sure, maybe a surround sound system too," Phil answered sarcastically. "Let me think for a minute… NO!"

"Aw, just kiddin' man, but you never get anything in life if you don't ask, right?" He knelt down and searched in his bag for another can of paint.

"Sure you do, Mal. You stand in line and pay for it at the register like everybody else." He hesitated. "Where you goin' after you stop defacing public property?"

"Home, man, why? You wanna meet up for a beer?"

"Yeah, there's a hottie workin' in video games, and we were thinkin' about hookin' up later. She asked me if I had a friend. You know, she's gotta friend, I gotta friend? You, my man, are the friend. You in?"

Mal was checking the latest element in his mural as he considered Phil's offer. "Does hair grow everywhere but where you want it to?"

"What the hell does that mean?"

"Some shit my baldheaded old man used to say. Translation: yeah, I'm in, but this one better not be a barker 'cause I hate the smell of dog food on a chick's breath in the morning." He was already gathering his equipment when he ended the call.

Twenty-Four

The light on Emily's side of the bed was on. She seemed fully absorbed in her new paperback novel. John enjoyed watching the expression on her face change as she turned another page. She always looked sexy at this time of the night, even if she was in her sweats. To him, she was the most beautiful woman in the world. Whenever he said it out loud, her typical response was, "Love really is blind, isn't it, honey?"

Even when she said things like that, he still knew better. She had saved his ass on their first camping trip, killing the monster trying to make a meal out of him, but there was so much more. She also rescued his idea of what real love could be. To think that any woman would be willing to sacrifice herself like that, going against every natural instinct to run, it was something he wouldn't expect his own mother to do. Emily had stuck around to fight for someone like… him. In his mind, she was the epitome of perfection. Nothing could shake that.

Then he smelled it. At first, he thought he was having a sensory recollection of the alien stench of that day in the woods. Then he ruffled the blanket and caught it full on. Unfortunately, taken by surprise, John started to cough uncontrollably.

"Sorry, honey. I guess it was the pizza," she apologized without taking her eyes from her book. "Whew, that was worse than I thought."

He laughed out loud. A big whooping laugh. He couldn't help himself. He had just been thinking about how sexy she was and now… Now, the look on her face was stern, and he needed a cover. He alternated between fake coughs and stifled laughing. In the end, she could not maintain the façade of disapproval. She started laughing too.

Finally composing themselves, Emily dropped another bomb. This time it was a return to the haunted house conversation. "You know, when I was at that house earlier, those cats I told you about were different from any cats I had ever seen before. I mean they looked like… demon cats. It was freaky."

"Demon cats? I thought hell was guarded by demon dogs." John was trying to be polite. He really wasn't interested in conversation just then.

"Well, I know in those movies you like, they always have dogs, Dobermans, but man, these cats… It was disturbing." Her book lay open-side down on the night table.

"Try not to think about it, Em. We should get some sleep." No sooner had he said it than he realized it was the wrong thing to say.

"How can you sleep, John? I mean, seriously… in the middle of the conversation? If I thought those cats were just my imagination, maybe I could go to sleep. Unfortunately for me, I now know that aliens are real. I know that people can hear their dead relatives talking, and some box can rip a person's spirit right out of their bodies. Next up, fucking demon cats. What's next?" She ran her fingers through her hair, brushing it away from her face. "You know it's real, John. You just can't roll over and pretend it's not."

"Yeah, honey, I know. We're probably going to discover a lot of other stuff out there in this kind of business. What do you want me to do?"

"You don't have to *do* anything, John. Just stay awake and hear me out."

"Well, it makes me feel like I *need* to do something, that's all. If you don't feel good about this job, then we don't have to take it. I know we need the money, but is it really worth having you stress out like this just to pay the bills?"

She was giving him *the look*. "Yes, in fact I really want to do this." Her voice carried no uncertainty.

"Okay, now I'm confused. One minute you're complaining about demon cats, the next, you seem adamant about taking this job." John's phone began to ring. "Who the hell is calling at this hour?"

"Maybe it's an emergency call. You know, like, *Hello, can someone help me? There's a demon cat gnawing on my leg.*" She paused to see whether he would reach for it. "You should answer it."

"I don't know who it is but, at this hour, they can leave a message. It's probably a wrong number anyway."

The phone stopped ringing as the call went to voicemail. John watched as the light of the display went dark again.

Twenty-Five

Mid-afternoon the following day, John finally noticed that someone had left him a message. Walking back to the office from the coffee shop on the corner, it occurred to him that his phone hadn't rung all day. He was concerned that he may have missed a call from Emily. He gritted his teeth when he saw the missed call. Pressing the message play button, he held the phone to his ear.

"John, it's Frank." He seemed excited. "It's incredible, man, so don't panic 'cause I think this is gonna work, but just in case…" There was a loud buzzing sound in the background. "Just in case anything goes wrong… look, if you don't hear from me by tomorrow morning, come by the house and check on me." John was getting that uneasy feeling in his gut. "Remember when you guys were here and I programmed you into the security system? Well, you have full access and… hang on a sec…"

John continued to hear the buzz in the background and something that sounded like metal clinking. Frank came back to the phone. "My computer lab is across from the elevator that goes to the armory. You can access it with the same security, so if you don't hear from me by morning, uh, come and see if there is anything you can do to… I guess… rescue my ass." His laughter was interrupted by an unidentifiable sound as the message cut off.

Stunned, John sat down on a nearby bus bench as the message ended. He played it through again to be sure that he had heard it right. He was listening intently when a bus pulled up and stopped, its engine drowning out Frank's words. The door swung open and the driver sat waiting.

Irritated, John waved him on so he could hear the message again. What the hell was Frank up to that he had to tell someone to come and check on him, to see if he was… what… alive?

He decided to call Paulie. Paulie was a hacker and if there was any kind of computer-related incident, he would be the best person to help. Besides Paulie had worked for Frank off and on during the last couple of years, so he would be more familiar than John when it came to security in and around the house and any issues that might develop. He woke his phone again and clicked through the contacts to find Benino, Paulie's last name.

After a few rings, there was an answer, "You got Paulie."

"Hey Paulie, this is John."

"Hazard, whassup?"

"Well, I'm not quite sure. I got a call from Frank, I guess it was last night… yeah, 'cause me and Em were… anyway he left a message."

"What'd he say? You sound worried."

"Well, he said, if I didn't hear from him by morning to come over to his place and check on him."

"Right, so did you?"

"Well, no, I just got the message. I'm gonna head over there in about a half hour, and I was wondering if you could meet me there."

"Need somebody to hold your hand there, John?"

"No, but I think whatever's going on might have something to do with… He was calling from his computer lab. I could hear some… I guess they were electrical sounds in the message. I thought maybe you could help me out if that's the case."

"Sure, man, no problem. I was just messin' with you, right? I get off work at five. I can meet you at Frank's by six, cool?"

"Okay. I would tell you to bring some tools or something with you, but I wouldn't know what that would be."

"I got a laptop with me if I need it, and I'll bring a hammer just in case."

"Right. You're really going to use a hammer to work on a computer?"

"No, John, the hammer's for your stupid ass!"

"Oh, you're hilarious, Paulie. Just be there?"

"I'll be there. Then you can tell me what you and the little lady were doin' when you missed the call. I'm guessin' you was…"

"No, man, we were talking!"

Paulie laughed. "I'll see you there. I'm all hot and shit now, talking 'bout your no-sex life!" He laughed again and ended the call.

Twenty-Six

John was sitting in the driveway when Paulie pulled up to the house. Listening to talk radio made him wonder what was going on in the world. It seemed to him that things were getting crazy, and most of the world's population didn't even seem to notice or care. He believed that ultimately it had something to do with supernatural forces. The classic battle of Good and Evil had the world and our government in turmoil, including the local cops and crooks. Were they all just the same people in different uniforms?

John knew there were forces at work that most did not understand. Even people making a living off spiritual shit didn't know, or at least they couldn't say why the turmoil seemed to be escalating. That didn't mean he had to accept things as they are, just that he had to live in the same world with it, whether he liked it or not. What other option was there? He figured if he wanted to escape the craziness of this world, death was probably the only way out, and it had its own repercussions.

As Paulie got out of his car, John turned off the radio and called out, "Hey, Pauliana, what's up?"

"What? You a fuckin' comedian now? You called me, remember?" Paulie appeared ready for a fight until he cracked a wide smile. "Just messing with you, man. Let's get in there and find out what Frank's been playin' with."

John got out of his car as Paulie walked up to the house still talking, and ranting. "I gotta tell you, John, if he's got some naked supermodel in there, drinking champagne outta her shoe or somethin', and he ain't answering the phone cause he's tearin' it up... either I'm gonna kick his ass or demand seconds. Maybe both if he gives us some shit."

They stood at the door while John put his hand on the scanner to unlock the door. "I hear ya, and I'm in on that, at least the ass kickin' part. You can have the seconds, man, I got all I need at the house."

Paulie shook his head. "Lucky stiff."

The door lock made very little sound as it slid to the unlocked position, and he heard a voice say, "Welcome back, John. We've missed you."

"Ain't that the shit!" Paulie was grinning.

"Yeah, I know. It probably knows how long it's been since the last time I was here."

"So how is she anyway?" Paulie followed John through the doorway into the large foyer.

"Who, the chick in the security recording? I don't know, Paulie, I've never met…"

"Nah, dumbass. Emily." Paulie shoved John as they moved through the foyer and down the hall where the painting covered the elevator to the lower floor.

"Oh, she's great. She's been working on getting the business going and got us our first job, a haunted house. We're supposed to clean the ghosts out of it. Get this, demon cat ghosts."

Paulie laughed at that. He was checking around for any sign of Frank or maybe that supermodel. John headed down the other hall and stopped in front of the large painting on the wall.

"We goin' to the range?" Paulie asked as he came up from behind him. "I could use some practice."

"No, Frank said to go to his lab across from the elevator, but I don't remember anything across from the elevator on the first floor." He scratched his head.

"Across from the elevator? You think it's that one?" Paulie pointed at a normal sized painting hanging on the wall a few feet further down the hall, and went to check it out.

"It's got a hand," he said, placing his hand on the painting. Nothing happened. "I guess the house babe doesn't recognize me."

"Give me some space so I can try."

John stepped up and placed his hand on the painting. There were sounds coming from behind the wall but no sign of a seam or crack. Suddenly, a large section of the wall began to depress. About three inches back, it smoothly disappeared into the wall to the left. The room before them was dark until John stepped inside. The lights flickered on and lit up the lab.

"Holy shit!" John was speechless as he took in the scene before him.

"I ain't never seen so much tech in a room this small," Paulie exclaimed as he walked toward the large bank of computers and monitors. "And look at that! Whoa!" He was pointing at the precious metal framework of the machine. There were giant amethysts on stands. The crystals pointed at the blackened wall.

"What is all this stuff, Paulie? That there looks like some ancient art piece, and…" John whistled. "Look at these computers. Sure is a lot of high–end equipment."

"Did Frank say anything about any of this in his message?" Paulie was still staring at one of the monitors and the elaborate screen saver running on it.

"No, man. Nothin' about it." John moved to the desk and noticed Frank's pistol lying right where he had left it. "Maybe he didn't want us to know about this unless there was some kind of problem," he said, holding up the gun to show Paulie. "You know, like, if he got himself in trouble, which he obviously did."

"Well, looks like he did get his ass in a crack. Now we gotta pry him out." Paulie sat down in Frank's chair and pulled the Post-it note from the monitor. "Send No Angel, what the fuck?" He held the small yellow square up for John to see it. "John, I gotta bad feeling about this. I think Frank is on a... this is gonna sound crazy dude, but I think this is the password here."

John leaned forward waiting for Paulie to finish the sentence, "You think Frank's on some kind of mission?"

"Yeah, that's exactly what I think." Paulie got up and walked to the wall. He ran his hand over its blackened surface.

"If he's gone somewhere, why didn't he call us? Why did he tell us to come here?"

Paulie turned around to face John. "Dude..." He pointed at the wall. "I, uh, I think he's in there. If this is what I think it is, we need to get the guys together, and we need to do it fast." He swiped his hand back over his hair and sat back down in front of the computer ready to power it up.

"What the hell are you talking about?" John was obviously confused.

"John, call Clark and tell him Frank needs us. Tell him to get hold of the other guys and get 'em here quick. Tell him to have them bring any trophies they brought back from Iraq. Don't worry, he'll know what you're talking about." He spun around to face the monitor again. "And you better call Emily and get her over here. Otherwise, she's gonna flip out if we're gone for a couple of days."

John was dumbfounded. He stared over Paulie's shoulder as he switched on the computer and started typing, SEND_NO_ANGEL, in all caps just as Frank had written it. The bank of eight monitors sprung to life, each screen awash with multi-colored graphs, charts and some calculations that neither of them had ever seen before. When he saw the red box on the screen flashing in front of Paulie with four words, John suddenly started to catch up to what Paulie had been trying to tell him. The message read *"Power Surge: Connection Terminated."*

Twenty-Seven

Emily's phone was ringing. Checking her caller ID, she was glad to see that it was John. "Hey! Where are you? I was getting worried." Glancing at the time, she saw that it was around eight thirty. He recognized the genuine relief of a woman who had seen a lot of craziness in the short time they'd known each other. She was keenly aware that the worst really could happen. "I've been trying to call you for almost two hours."

"Sorry, Em. I think the walls here in Frank's lab are shielded. I'm guessing the signal can't get through. I didn't even notice the voicemail until I tried calling you."

"Did you say Frank's lab? Frank, as in *our* Frank?"

"Yeah, I met Paulie here at Frank's after work, and I…"

"You didn't even call and tell me you were going there!"

"Right, well…"

"Well, my ass, John Hazard. I know you. If you're there, something is going on. I think you better tell me about it, like, two hours ago."

"Yeah, I know, but I didn't know, you know?"

"Know what, for crying out loud?

"Know what I would find when I got here. That's what I'm trying to say. I got this… well, remember last night when…"

"Spit it out, John. What the hell's going on?"

John took a breath before starting. "Remember last night when the phone rang? We were in bed."

"Yes, I remember. You didn't answer it even though I told you to?" She had that scolding mom tone in her voice that drove him crazy and made him feel like a kid who'd been caught feeding his peas to the dog under the table.

"Damn! Okay, so you were right, I should have, but…"

"And, it was Frank. And he's in some kind of trouble, and we gotta rescue his ass, right?"

"Uh, how did you know all that?"

"Look. John, we haven't been together all that long, but I've been with you long enough to know that when one of your friends is involved, it's probably gonna be some crazy life or death situation. Remember what was going on when I met him?" She took a breath. "Ever since then, most of our dealings with Frank have been pretty crazy. Don't you think?"

"Well, I don't…"

"Come on. You agree, right, John?" Her tone intensified, but still, she had to wait for his answer.

"I guess so." He sounded a bit defeated, and she knew she had him.

"Okay then. Tell me what you need me to bring and where to bring it." Emily eased up and assumed a gentler tone. She figured he was probably dealing with some crisis. Whatever was going on, she hoped he would start to figure out that calling her when something important was going on, or if he was going to be late, was the least he could do.

Meantime, John sighed with relief and fed her the list of supplies. When he had finished, he asked, "You mad at me? Because you know I didn't plan this. I don't even know for sure what *this* is."

"I know, we can talk about it when I get there. You take care. I'm on my way… and John… I love you."

"Love you too. Be careful. I'll see you soon." As soon as the call ended, he opened his contact list and scrolled to Clark.

"Clark here," came the cheerful voice at the other end of the line.

"Hey. It's John." There was no response so he added, "Hazard."

"Yeah, hey, what's up, John? It's been a while. Everything okay? I mean… you know what I mean."

"Well, as far as Em and me are concerned, everything is cool. It's Frank."

"Frank?" Clark was surprised that Frank would be in any kind of trouble. He always thought that guys like him could afford to buy their way out of anything. "What's our millionaire game developer up to that has you calling me? Doesn't have anything to do with the warehouse does it?"

"Not the warehouse. Well, I don't think so anyway. Honestly, man, I really don't know. He left a message on my phone to come here if I didn't hear from him, so Paulie and me are here at his house. There's this… Well, of course, he has a state of the art computer lab, but what's really strange, there's this machine in it. I mean, I really don't know what it is, some kind of contraption, I guess. I'm not sure what we're facing here, but Frank needs our help."

"Right, so when do you need me?"

"As soon as you and the guys can get here. How long do you think it will take to round them up?"

"What time is it? Damn, John, its almost nine o'clock. Wait,   " Clark paused, "You said the guys? All of the guys?"

"Right, Paulie said you'd have their numbers, so can you call them? We need them here ASAP."

"I don't know if I can get them all, but I'll leave messages if necessary. We'll be there soon. Hang tight."

"One more thing, Clark. Paulie says to tell the guys to bring all the trophies from Iraq."

"Trophies… oh shit, for real? Exactly what did you find at Frank's?"

"Some kind of secret computer lab and a strange machine, it looks ancient, built from gold and…"

"He actually built that thing?" Clark's voice took on a tone of dread.

"You know about the crystal machine? What is it?"

"Listen, John, I don't know what it is or what it does. Look I… we'll tell you the whole story when we get there. I need to get this thing going. No worries, we'll be there soon."

"But…" was all he got out before Clark ended the call.

Twenty-Eight

When Emily arrived just after ten, John was standing on the steps waiting for her as she pulled up. He started toward the car while she was still getting her things together. Not always the gentleman, this time he opened the door for her. "Hey there, wild thing!" He wanted to be as upbeat as possible considering the situation. Maybe she would go easy on him if he kept things on a positive note.

"Really? Wild thing? Seriously, John, we should be laying on the couch watching *Ghost Squad* right now, not getting ready to do some crazy rescue mission." She pulled the trunk release, slid out of the seat, and slammed the door.

"Did I say it was a rescue mission?"

"Look, Mr. Mysterious, if this isn't a rescue mission, then I brought the wrong gear." She reached into the trunk and grabbed one of the straps of the backpack, lifting it out. "I just hope we aren't gone more than a couple of days, because I only left enough food for Ralphie to last that long." She handed him the backpack and reached for the second one. "I didn't load these to the max. I figured we would need to pack in some ammo or…"

He had set the backpack on the ground and was pulling her toward him. Involuntarily, she let go of the other pack and turned to face him. In his eyes, she could read his concern. She softened her stance.

"Look," he started, putting his arms around her and kissing her forehead before beginning again. "I don't know what I'm headed into here, or even how to plan for it. I can't even say if we'll make it back from this one, so I can't let you go with me on this one, Em."

She stiffened in his arms, "*Let* me go? Right! Look here, John Hazard, you are in no position to *let* me do anything." She had instantly transformed from a caring, loving partner to Medusa in tight jeans in two seconds flat, and the snakes on her head were out for blood. "We live together, have a business together and, at the moment at least, we are in this life together. Even with all of that, you are *NOT* nor will you *EVER BE* my boss. I do not require your permission to do anything, understand?"

He was taken off guard by the vehemence of her reaction, but he did understand. After all, she'd been through a lot already with aliens up in the woods and thugs who had threatened her life. He felt sorry that...

"And don't go thinking that I must be overwhelmed with everything I've been through, either, John." She mocked him with an overly sympathetic tone. "I have a vested interest in your ass, and I'm damn sure going along to help protect it. Whatever it takes!"

She'd done this before, reading his thoughts like that. He couldn't figure out how she did it, but he could see her point. She certainly had proved herself in the past. After all, he might not have made it back from the field trip without her. How could he say anything but, "That's what I like about you, Em. I never have to guess at what you're thinking. You just lay it right out there."

"Damn right! Now how about you help me with this backpack." She thrust the pack at him and he grabbed it before it hit the ground. Slamming the trunk closed, she snatched the pack from him and headed toward the door.

He stood for a second watching her, admiring her ass in those jeans, his mind wandering for a moment. *How could I even consider leaving her here and doing this thing without her? Shit! Am I... pussy whipped?*

"No!" he said out loud, trying to convince himself. He followed her up the steps and through the door. Neither of them noticed the black SUV coming up the drive behind them.

"Which way?" she asked once they were in the foyer.

"The lab is right across the hall from the elevator. Paulie's in there, so go ahead. I think I see headlights outside, and I want to be there to greet whoever just pulled up."

John headed back out and stood in the driveway as the lights of the SUV turned off. All four doors opened at once. Archer, Joe, Max and Charles piled out of the truck. "Do you guys live together or what? You got here fast!"

They all headed to the tailgate as Archer responded, "In these crazy times… earthquakes, tsunamis, hurricanes, tornados … Hell, people are always talkin' about the end of the world. We don't talk. We prepare for it."

Charles added, "You didn't hang with us much after Iraq, John Boy. We made a pact to stay in touch, stay informed, and stay ready."

Max chimed in, "Besides, dude, after the crazy shit we got into over there, who knows what kind of mayhem could happen, and at any time."

"What kind of crazy shit?" John felt like he was the only one who didn't know what they were talking about.

"You never heard about the chamber?" Joe asked.

"No, I guess you guys are good at keeping secrets. Anybody wanna clue me in?"

"Okay, Hazard. Let's go inside. It's important that we talk about this before we run into God knows what and get our asses kicked." Archer was the voice of impending doom, and he looked serious.

"So, how's that girl of yours taking this, um, rescue mission thing? Have you told her what you're up to?" Max doubted it, even as he asked.

"Oh, well, I didn't tell her the details yet, but I'm sure once we get a briefing, she'll be thrilled." He was being sarcastic.

"She's here?" Joe sounded excited.

"Oh, yeah, and she's planning on going with…"

Max cut him off, "You aren't going to let her go, are you?"

"Right, uh… you might not want to put it that way around her. She's pretty stubborn when it comes to shit like that."

"No way, John. No fuckin' way. We might be gettin' into some bad Juju, and it sure as hell won't be no place for a lady." Joe was looking at John as if it were *his* decision whether Emily should go. *If only he knew.*

John stopped and faced the group. "Guys, look, I know that Em might look small and even a bit helpless compared to you apes but, believe me, when she's pissed off, you do *not* want to push her. I've seen what she can do when she's angry, and somewhere up north there's a dead fuckin' alien corpse that could testify to that."

"Yeah, well, when she hears the Iraq story, maybe she'll rethink that stubborn chick thing." Archer laughed. "She might be crazy…" John glared at him. "About you of course, buddy, but she's not stupid. I'm sure she'll see it our way."

John wore half a grin as he shook his head and challenged, "I got a hundred dollar bill says, no matter what you say, you won't be able to talk her out of it."

"I'm in!" said Max, and the rest followed right behind, taking him up on what they saw as a sure bet.

"Right, let's go talk to her then, and you can brief us on this so-called 'Iraq Thing'." He smiled and led them down the hall to the lab, thoughts of what he could do with a couple hundred bucks creeping into his head.

Twenty-Nine

As the group entered the lab, there was a round of "Holy shit!" and "Fuck me!" as well as various other exclamations and profanities. Paulie was still sitting at the computer with Emily bending over the back of his chair to get a look over his shoulder. She turned to face them when she heard the commotion.

"Hey, guys!"

She sounded unusually cheerful. John scratched his head. This was a total disconnect from her earlier demeanor. She looked over at John who was stupefied to see her new attitude.

"You're not going to believe it, John. Paulie opened the portal while you were outside. We really need to go to the armory."

"What? How?" John tried to see past Paulie and check out whatever was on the screen. "Where?"

"There," she said, pointing to the large blackened rectangle on the wall. "When he turns that thing on, it opens up like a garage door. We could drive a car through it if we could get one in here." She grabbed his arm to make sure she had his full attention. "But that's not the worst. When that thing is open, it smells so bad, and I mean *bad*. As soon as it closes, the smell is gone."

John walked over to the sandstone wall and ran his hand over the rough surface as she continued, "It was the smell of death, John, and I know what that's like. I had some experience with that when one of my neighbors passed and they didn't find him for weeks. It's a very distinct smell."

"Yes, Em, I know. I had plenty of experience with it as a detective."

"Sorry, of course. Anyway, I think we're going to need all the weapons we can carry... and maybe gas masks."

Max was checking out the computer screen while the other guys were inspecting the discolored area on the wall. "Paulie, whatcha got?"

Paulie spun around in his chair to face him. "I'm not quite sure what it is, or where it goes." Frustration flashed across his face as he pointed at the wall. "I *can* tell you that the portal will only stay open for about five minutes at a time. Longer than that and this bitch starts to go critical. I'm guessin' Frank went through to investigate when the system reset, trapping him on the other side," adding in a low tone, "and God only knows where that thing goes."

"Shit! We need some kind of plan. Before we go, we better decide on a synced time when the gate will open for us to come back." Max rubbed his chin, looking at the wall.

Archer cautioned, "Right, but first we need to do a test. For all we know, there's a cliff on the other side, or maybe it's a vacuum. Hell, we could go through there and end up hanging off the dark side of Mars. I've read stories about wormholes and shit."

"So what would you suggest?" John was open to any ideas.

Clark had come in late without announcing himself, but now weighed in. "How about we tie a rope to something and toss it through?" He stood in the doorway, his arms stretched up to reach the doorframe above. "We could use a chair or anything with a little weight to it. Then we tie a rope to it, and push it through. If there's a drop off, we should be able to tell. If it vaporizes we'll know for sure, and then this is over 'cause then Frank is dust."

"I like that idea." Emily made damn sure to give her input. These guys were like family to her now, and she wasn't about to lose them to some foolishness like charging into hell without trying to find out if there was at least a chance to survive. "Somebody get a chair, and there's some rope over there on that counter. Let's do this, guys. I'm afraid Frank may be running out of time."

John headed for the rope, "Damn! We need to get this going and stop talking about it."

Phillip took the initiative. "I'll get a chair from the dining room." He ran down the hallway toward Frank's large dining room.

Archer expressed his concern, "Okay, this chair thing is a good plan, but we still haven't discussed Iraq, and what we might be getting into here."

"Are you going to tell this story or what, Arch? I think we deserve to know the truth." John turned to face him.

Archer began pacing. "Somebody else should tell it. I mean, we all know what happened to a certain degree, but since it went down, I think some have figured out some more aspects to the story."

Charles agreed. "Well, this machine here proves that Frank knows a hell of a lot more than we do, right? Before we open that thing up and throw a fucking chair through, we need to get it all out in the open."

"I totally agree, Charles. I have no idea what you all are talking about." Emily stood with her hand on her hip.

John stepped in. "Archer, why don't you start? Fill us in on what you know. If the rest of you have something to add, feel free to jump in at any time."

Just then, Phillip came back into the room with his prize, one of the ornate chairs that usually sat around the giant dining table in the Chow Hall, as Frank called it. "I got the chair, so let's do it."

"Not yet, dude," said Paulie. "We gotta talk some mission details first."

"Yes, you do." Emily reached out. "How about you hand me that chair, Phil. I might as well sit down for this." She caught hold of the chair as Phillip slid it across the floor.

"Okay. Tell us your story, guys, and you should probably make it quick. Frank's expecting us." John was growing impatient.

Thirty

"Max, you wanna go first?" Archer was hoping he would take the lead. "I think you're probably the best storyteller here. I'd probably be pumping it up too much if I told it." The others nodded, and Max blushed at the compliment. He wasn't used to being in the spotlight.

"Okay, sure, but you guys fill the gaps if I forget anything." He took a deep breath and released it before beginning. "I don't know about you guys, but I have nightmares about that day." He leaned back against the wall. "Okay, it went down like this..."

***

That morning, the Alpha Two squad met for a briefing on the details of the mission:

"There have been reports of enemy snakes, a pocket of 'em right here in the southern outskirts of the city." The commander slapped the pointer against the map as he spoke. "Reliable sources claim ten to fifteen insurgents. We need to investigate with extreme caution and exterminate with extreme prejudice if the reports are indeed accurate."

He aimed the pointer at Frank. "DeMint, I need you to take your squad, two hummers, and a fifty cal. Go clean it up." He circled an area on the map with a red marker as he spoke.

"Sir, can we expect aerial support on this picnic if necessary?" Frank stood at ease with his hands behind his back.

"All ya gotta do is phone home, ET, and the saucer will be there to fly you out. But, I know you Frank, if anybody's gonna need backup, it'll be the sorry bastards you're going after. Now get your skinny asses out of here, and get to work!" Frank's squad tried to suppress their laughter.

"Yes, sir!" Frank saluted and turned on his heels to leave.

"One last thing, DeMint," the commander called after him. "Rumor is they've been working overtime putting out IEDs in that area, so keep frosty. You get me?"

"Yes sir, like ice." Frank called over his shoulder as his team exited the briefing quarters.

"Fuckin' IEDs," grumbled Paulie. "Why these bastards can't just get out there and duke it out like real men? Gotta hide on some hill behind a rock a mile away with a cell phone and call it in."

"I guess 'cause maybe they don't have choppers with a-thousand-rounds-a-minute guns mounted on them," Charles answered sarcastically as they walked back to the barracks to get their gear together.

"I know you ain't makin' excuses for them sand-eatin' motherfuckers…" He skipped a beat and waited for a response before adding, "Right, Chucky?"

"I'm just saying, man. If we were back in the States and some punks invaded our turf, what would you do?" Charles was trying to offer some perspective.

Max saw his chance. "I think, if it was back in the States, it'd be over by now. Half the country would surrender to save their own ass, and the other half, the real patriots, the baddest asses the world has ever seen, would've stepped up and wiped the fuckers out already."

"Oorah, Marine!" Paulie cheered. "Don't mess..." He paused to give Max a hand slap before finishing. "...with the U.S."

"Man, let's hope we never have to find out what would really happen, right?" Charles knew it was futile to try to press his point. "Let's gear up."

"I'm glad you boys decided to kiss and make up because we've got a mission to complete, and I'd like to get back before dark. Now get your gear and meet me at the motor pool."

Frank always knew how to wrap up an argument between the guys. Sure, he knew it would come up again later in one form or another, but you can't walk on the edge of a sword everyday without a bit of conflict. He understood and was more than ready to deal with it.

Thirty-One

At 09:20, the team was gathered at the Humvees. As Joe finally joined them, Frank and the rest of the squad were chatting it up about their favorite greasy diner breakfasts and how they would kill to have some on a morning like this.

"'Bout fuckin' time, Joe! What took ya so long? Have to drop a load before you could get your head straight?" Charles got a big laugh out of the group with that one.

"I got a load for ya, bitch!" Joe said, grabbing hold of his crotch. "We ready to go?"

"Yeah, why don't you lead the prayer for us this morning, Father Joe, seein' as how you had more time to meditate on the message than the rest of us fellas?" Frank was taking a chance here. There was no telling how Joe would respond, especially on this particular morning.

"I can do that."

Joe stepped up as the nine men formed a circle and each one bowed his head, holding his flak helmet with both hands.

"Morning, Lord. As we head out this morning, I want to thank you for all your blessings on this here unit. I know we're undeserving and all, but to protect the good folks around here we gotta get out there and kill some more of these bastards."

He cleared his throat before going on, "And Lord, as your servants, we understand our mission is to punch the tickets, validate the parking, and send these fools straight to hell. We know our mission and why you send no angel to do the devil's work. Oorah!"

"Oorah!" came the response.

"I guess you weren't shittin' us, Joe. That was mighty impressive!" Frank said.

"No problem, cap'n." Joe smiled as he put on his helmet and adjusted the strap.

"Alright, let's get 'em up and move 'em out." Frank waved his arm in a circle like a cowboy twirling a lasso in the Old West. "We got some work to do." With that, the team piled into the large vehicles and headed for the security gate.

Thirty-Two

As the Humvees reached the outer edge of the populated area where the base was situated, traffic suddenly came to a halt. Apparently, there had been an accident involving a motorcycle and a pickup truck. The truck had been loaded way beyond its capacity with crates of scrawny chickens. They must have been stacked several feet above the top of the cab. Pieces of smashed crates and scraps of wood were scattered around the area. Confused and excited, the birds were making their escape, and some of the locals were trying to apprehend them.

Paulie, who was driving the lead vehicle, spoke into his headset. "Hey guys, we got a situation here. Seems a motorcycle tried to jump a chicken truck. Mohammad Evil Knieval is down and kickin'. Chickens everywhere. Advise."

Frank tried to assess from where he was sitting, but it was difficult to make out the entire scene from that vantage point. "Are you able to scan the rooftops and windows ahead from your position?" he asked.

"Yah, that's a big affirmative, sir. Appears to be clear."

"Me and Ingram are coming up. Stand ready."

Frank fastened the strap on his helmet and pulled back the action on his M-14 before opening the door. With a nod to Clark, he stepped out and walked toward the scene ahead cautiously scanning the buildings on either side of the road. Clark was right behind him as they neared the front of the first vehicle. From there, they could take in the mayhem. The driver of the chicken truck seemed very upset and continued to yell at the motorcycle rider.

Frank spoke into his comm. "Looks clear. Gonna help these assholes move out of the street."

Clark knew a few words in Arabic, so he tried to communicate to the truck driver what they were about to do. Unfortunately, his language skills were a little shaky and he ended up telling the driver, "We are also half the man, get out short," to which the driver responded with a blank stare.

Clark tried again, wording it differently this time. "I, my friend, fly rooster man. Kick that crate and marker." The driver shook his head and held his arms above his head as if surrendering.

"What did you say to him?" Frank asked Clark who was now at a loss.

"I thought I told him we would move the motorbike and the other guy out of the way so we could pass, and they could work it out later."

"Obviously, he didn't hear it that way," Frank said as he grabbed the handles of the motorcycle and dragged it out of their path. He walked back to the rider calling to Clark, "Keep an eye on things while I get this guy out of the street."

Just then, a shot rang out. The driver of the chicken truck was hit in the shoulder and spun around by the impact of the slug. He dropped into the dust covering the road in a mist of blood as he lost his hold on the chicken he had been carrying. Immediately, the bird scurried away squawking in panic.

Frank had just reached the injured man when another shot rang out. He grabbed the guy by the arm and began pulling him toward the safety of the armed vehicles. He would only need to move him a few feet to get him out of view of the sniper.

Meanwhile, in the lead Humvee, Joe slid back the roof panel and released the lock on the turret holding the fifty cal in place. He yelled at Clark, "Where?"

Clark yelled back into his comm, "Rooftop, two o'clock."

There was a loud clack-acking sound as the fifty roared to life. Not taking any chances, Joe strafed across the length of the rooftop. He believed the wall was thin enough to shoot through it to hit the sniper.

Frank had returned to the crash scene where he pulled the rider clear and tucked him into a recess in a nearby wall. With the man safely out of the line of fire, he ran back to the driver of the pickup. Dragging him over to where the other guy was hiding, he leaned him back against the stone wall.

"Hang in there, buddy," he told the man as he unzipped a pouch on his belt and pulled out a square gauze bandage. He pressed it against the driver's wound, using the man's own hand to hold it in place. Frank attempted to indicate to the man that he needed to keep pressure on it.

As he checked to be sure that it was safe to go back to the Hummer, he saw that the motorcycle rider was helping the wounded trucker. He nodded his approval glad to see that the two seemed to be forgetting their differences for the moment.

A shot rang out from the rooftop striking the fender of the front vehicle, and again Joe laid a line of fire down the side of the short wall that shielded the sniper. This time he got lucky. A cloud of red mist above the wall was a good indication that someone's bullet had found its mark. He grunted in satisfaction and pummeled the spot with more lead just to make sure. Satisfied that the shooter was dead or severely incapacitated, he yelled, "Clear!"

Before they could maneuver the Humvees past the wreck, however, they would need to move the truck out of the way. No need to be concerned about the crates, they would roll right over them.

Frank kept watch while Clark got behind the wheel of the truck. The engine was still idling so he threw it into gear. Gravel flew creating a dust cloud as he backed it out of the road. He shut it down and jumped out, tossing the keys to the injured driver. Before the keys had dropped to the ground, Clark and Frank were running for the Humvee.

"Go! Go!" Max yelled at Paulie, signaling him to get moving when he saw that everyone was in. Paulie ground the gears and they lurched forward glad to be on their way once again.

Thirty-Three

About five clicks outside the village, there were very few buildings in sight. The squad was on high alert, watching for any sign of activity especially to the right in the rolling hills. It was quite common for the insurgents to hide in the foothills using cell phones to activate roadside bombs. A flash, a reflection of light, even the slightest movement could indicate that someone was there. Sometimes they would hide in plain sight. Unfortunately, in their world, everyone was expendable. Even a woman or child could be carrying a bomb or the detonator. Often they were killed by their own improvised devices.

There was no sign of life today, however. Not in the hills, not on the road, not anywhere to be seen. Paulie held the speed of the Humvee steady at sixty kilometers per hour. At that rate, he figured they would reach their destination in about an hour. There was the usual light banter in the cab in spite of the fact they had just escaped a grave situation. Humor helped them to cope with the craziness in this place where anything but loss of life was considered a win.

Driving along, Paulie got to thinking about a girl back home. No reason, really. She just popped into his mind. He smiled remembering the night he had spent with her. To say he was daydreaming would be an understatement. He could see her there so clearly. Taking a deep breath, he smelled the sweet scent of her. The memory was so vivid that he was damn near astral projected out of his body.

Suddenly, an IED exploded nearby with an earsplitting WHARUMP. Instantly, Paulie's reflexes kicked in and he slammed on the brakes. The Humvee skidded to a stop just beyond the site of the explosion. The second vehicle slid to a stop behind him sending up a cloud of blue gray smoke as rubber melted on the surface of the road.

"Holy shit!" Frank yelled into his comm, "Is everybody okay up there?"

Except for their ears ringing from the blast, everyone was intact and uninjured. Although he was unable to understand what Frank was asking, Max assumed he would want an assessment and responded with a brief casualty report. "No injuries here, but ears ringing for sure. Can anybody see anything?" His ears felt as though they were bleeding.

Phillip backed their vehicle away from the lead Humvee on Frank's orders. He could not afford to have both vehicles destroyed should there be another explosion. The team scanned the hills for any sign of insurgents, and Joe slid up into the turret and readied the fifty cal. Taking hold of the grips, he turned slowly panning the area for any trouble.

Frank was poised to exit the truck to check on the other men when the ground began shaking. "What the fuck?" was all he managed to say as the earth swallowed the heavy armored truck ahead of them.

Paulie was checking his ears for seepage with one hand and gripping the wheel of the vehicle with the other when the Humvee was swallowed up in the sinkhole. Still shaken by the explosion, they hit bottom with a jolt that nearly knocked him out. He could swear he had pissed himself as he felt a warm sensation spreading across his lap. Sand, rocks, and debris were scattered across the hood and clinging to the windshield.

Next to him in the passenger seat, Max was waving his arms and moving his mouth, but Paulie couldn't hear anything but the continued ringing in his ears. He knew he should be doing something. Instead, he just sat there.

Plunged into dark, everyone was disoriented. The truck had landed upright on its wheels, falling straight down into the deep hole. Though the impact had been partially absorbed by the Humvee's tires and chassis, there was obviously damage to the engine and steam was rising from beneath the hood. Streams of muted sunlight illuminated the swirling dust and sand that was falling from the gaping hole above.

Above ground, the rest of the crew piled out of the second vehicle. All but Joe, that is. He was manning the big gun and keeping an eye on the surrounding area as he continued to slowly turn in full circles, his finger hovering over the trigger.

"Be careful, guys," Frank warned, "The ground around that hole looks damn unstable. I don't need to have the rest of you falling in." Despite the warning, the men moved cautiously forward to the edge.

Meanwhile, Paulie and the guys below ground were gathering their wits about them and coming to grips with what had happened. It was apparent that they were sitting inside some kind of cavern or maybe some kind of man-made underground chamber. The IED probably weakened the ground above and they had dropped right through. But how were they going to get out of here? The light from above was not sufficient to get a good look around, so Paulie flipped on the headlights. "Holy shit!" He was staring at a large statue illuminated just in front of them.

"Weapons at the ready! Stay frosty." Max yelled, hoping the others could hear him over the dull buzz in their ears that continued to distort their senses. He opened the heavy door and stepped out of the truck, flipping the switch that turned on the light mounted on his rifle. The others got out after him and switched on their tactical lights. Each beam shot out in its own direction, cutting through the darkness like the blade of a long sword.

Up above, Frank was calling out to them. "Paulie, Max, anybody down there, do you copy?" There was nothing but static in response. He turned to Clark and hollered, "Get me a rope!"

Clark quickly headed back to the truck to dig through the gear and find the rope. He found a neat coil tucked in the back and ran back to Frank calling, "Got it!"

Frank took the rope and untied the knot that held it together. Then he made a loop for his foot so he could be lowered into the hole. "I'm going in," he told his crew. "You guys lower me in slowly. No matter what, don't get too close to the edge. Keep the rope tight and, whatever happens, don't let go. I'll give it three yanks when I need you to pull me back up. Give me 15 minutes. If you don't get a signal of some kind, get your asses out of here."

He looked at them squarely. "Keep an eye out for whoever set that IED off. They might still be out there somewhere, you got me?"

In unison they replied, "We got you, sir!"

As carefully as possible, Frank made his way to the opening in the ground before him. "I'm coming in!" he yelled down to anyone who might hear him. Without waiting for a response, he quickly tied a bandana scarf around his head to cover his face and protect himself from the fine sand billowing up from the dark hole.

Turning to face his crew, Frank called back, "Give me some tension!"

As the rope became taut, he stepped backward into the dusty void. He could hear someone calling to him, "Frank! We're over here. Check this out!" As he approached the floor of what appeared to be a large chamber, his eyes slowly adjusted to the darkness. Aside from the gaping hole above him, the only light in the cavern came from the beams cast by the truck's headlights along with the small handheld flashlights and tactical lights. Unfortunately, the light was dampened by the dust in the air.

As his feet touched the ground, a couple of guys came to meet him. "What the hell is this place?" Frank inquired, pulling a flashlight from his belt and shooting his own beam of light into the darkness as he switched it on.

"We don't know, man, but it definitely feels old and creepy down here. Check out the statue in front of the 'Vee. Talk about freaky shit!" Malcolm was shining his light in the direction of the truck.

Thirty-Four

"So that's what happened on the mission you guys were on when you lost the 'Vee?" John interrupted the story.

"Yeah," replied Archer. "We had to leave some of our gear down there too. No way we could get all of us and our gear into one truck to get back."

John looked at them incredulously. "I don't get it, guys. We hung out together that night, and you didn't say shit about any of this."

"Look, John," Max cut in, "We didn't tell *anybody* about this. We agreed to keep it on the down low because of the stuff we pulled out of there."

"What kind of stuff? Hurry and finish the story, we need to get going. We don't know what's going on with Frank," Emily blurted out.

"I think we should let Arch finish telling the rest of the story," Max answered in an ominous tone.

"Alright, Arch. You got us all up in that shit. You do it justice, man." Paulie encouraged him to go on.

Archer rubbed his hands together, took a deep breath, and got back to the story.

"Okay, so there we were, in this cave or chamber or whatever…"

***

Frank pulled the bandana down from his face as he walked around the dust-covered truck. His eyes scanned it for damage as he went along until he was standing between the beams of the headlights. The statue before him had the body and features of a man covered only by a loincloth, however, any human resemblance ended there.

There was a second pair of arms extending from its sides about twelve inches below the upper arms. Frank estimated the creature to be eight or nine feet tall as it hovered above him. "Holy shit, this is one big ugly sumbitch."

The sculpture had been crafted with intricate details to show rippling muscles and even small surface veins. The body appeared to be smooth and flawless. Even the head was huge, hairless and foreboding. However, regardless of how strange and unsettling the body of the creature was, it wasn't until Frank got a look at its face that he felt the chills run up his spine.

The being had a broad caveman-like forehead and a strong brow, but that wasn't what shocked him. It was the larger than normal single eye protruding from beneath the brow like a softball. Directly beneath the terrifying eye was a nose that was more like a hump with two large slits through which it was probably capable of taking in massive amounts of air.

Lastly, the mouth was definitely not human. It was more like that of an enormous feline, perhaps a strange hairless tiger, with a menacing set of jaws held partially open to expose its massive bone-crushing power. Its large curved fangs likely protruded when closed, and the rows of grinding molars behind them made it appear as though the hideous creature might be the perfect killing machine.

Frank shuddered at the thought of it getting hold of any part of his body. "This thing looks real, like it was in the middle of something and then froze somehow." He reached out his hand and touched one of the legs. "Oh shit!" he yelled, pulling his hand back as though he had touched a hot stove.

Malcolm stepped up beside him. "What is it, Frank?"

Pulling his weapon up with the business end pointed at the statue, Frank shouted, "This is no statue! The fucking thing is real!"

Charles began moving up closer. "Say what?"

"I touched its leg, and I assure you it is not made of stone. It felt like flesh." Frank was backing up now.

Archer yelled out, "My god, its eye just moved! I think it's watching you."

Max called out from across the chamber, "You mean to tell me that thing, whatever it is, is actually alive? Holy shit! I wonder how long it's been down here."

Paulie was aiming his rifle at its head. "You think it can move? We need to keep a guard on this motherfucker, or should I just shoot its ass and get it over with?"

"Okay, let's think about this." Frank had backed up to the front of the truck now. "You guys dropped down right in front of it with three tons of Humvee here, and it didn't as much as flinch? I think we should just leave the old bastard alone. As long as it's not threatening us, there's no reason to... uh, blast it to hell."

He kept his eyes riveted on the creature in front of him. "Besides, maybe he can give us a hand, or four, to lift this truck outta here." Chuckling nervously, he walked to the driver's side of the truck and reached in to turn off the engine. He decided to leave the lights on so they could better monitor the beast.

"Max, did you find anything over there? A tunnel or any way out so we can leave this shithole?" Frank walked toward him.

"No, sir. So far just some rolled up papers over there." He shone his light on what looked like a cabinet sitting next to some kind of table. Both were carved from stone.

"Paulie, keep an eye on that thing while I check this out." Frank headed toward the cabinet. "You guys split up and see what else is down here. We got ten minutes before the boys up top give up on hauling our asses out of here."

While the rest of the team searched the chamber for a way out or anything of interest, Frank checked out the cabinet, which seemed to be carved from a single piece of stone. There were several scrolls, each stored in its own square compartment. They could be ancient documents worth a fortune, or they could be newer and worth much less. Either way, he was not sure he should take the time to scrutinize them.

His heart was pounding just to think of the possibilities. Museums would pay a fortune for them if they proved to be ancient. The problem was to get them out of this hole and transport them without damage. Then, if they could get them back to the base, they would need to keep them someplace safe and secure. They would have to smuggle them through customs when they finally got a chance escape this shithole of a country and head home.

"Fuck me stupid!" came a voice from the other side of the chamber.

"Whatcha got?" came a reply from the shadows.

Archer had found something. With one hand, he was holding up what looked like a bag fashioned from the skin of an animal, and in the other hand was a fistful of gold coins. He beamed as the others walked up to him. "We are fuckin' rich!"

"Damn, look at that." Malcolm took one of the coins from Archer's hand and turned it over in the beam from his flashlight. "Man, I ain't never seen anything like this before. What do you think this says?" He handed the coin to Charles while Archer put the rest back in the bag and pulled on the leather strap to close it tightly.

Charles examined the coin. "Whoa. Seriously, this is big."

"What the fuck is it? Whatcha talking about over there?" Paulie yelled over his shoulder while keeping watch on the monster he was guarding.

Frank yelled back, "Not much, Paulie, except we found some bags of gold over here, and we are all about to be millionaires from the looks of it."

Paulie smiled and mumbled to himself, "Now that's what I'm talking about."

Thirty-Five

"So that explains how Frank got this mansion and started his business. I was wondering how he managed all that." John interrupted.

"Not really," Max spoke up. "The gold was only the beginning. It was more like what was in those documents that Frank brought back."

"You mean he brought back the scrolls and sold them to a museum?" Emily was surprised. "Usually ancient documents are donated, not sold."

"He didn't do either," Clark volunteered. "He hired someone to translate them."

"Yeah, and this machine here wasn't the only technology that came out of it." Paulie picked up the story. "There was some stuff that was so advanced that it took four guys from MIT to reverse engineer it. What they ended up with powerful enough that the government was trying to take it from Frank."

"Was it some kind of weapon?" John asked.

"I don't know exactly, but a big technology company snatched it up and paid Frank a pant load of cash just as the government was closing in on him. Last I heard, they were still being sued by the Justice Department to keep them from making it available to the public."

Paulie looked back to the screen in front of him as some kind of report began scrolling. "I just ran a diagnostic on the system. It'll be ready to run Frank's program again in about thirty. You guys need to be ready to go... Arch, finish your story. We got a little time."

"Okay, so there we were. We had found the gold and the scrolls, and then we found the bodies."

"Bodies? You mean dead people?" Emily was shocked now by the idea that the creature was found surrounded by bodies.

Archer wanted to get the story out so they could focus on getting Frank out of whatever predicament he had gotten himself in, so he continued.

***

This was a very large chamber, obviously built for some specific purpose, but there wasn't much there. Although they had found the cabinet and scrolls, this did not seem like a place where anyone would want to spend time. In fact, it seemed more like some kind of holding cell, or maybe a prison. It might have been a place where cattle, even people, could have been herded before a slaughter. After all, there was no apparent way to get in or out other than dropping in from above as they had.

In the darkness, beyond the odd creature that towered over the room, lay the remains of some thirty... people? These were not skeletons, but dried corpses, very well preserved as evidenced by the look of terror frozen on their faces.

"What the hell is this?" Malcolm yelled from beyond the lights of the Humvee. "Hey guys, I got bodies over here!" As the rest of the group headed toward him to see what he was talking about, Malcolm used his light to get a better look.

Archer came up behind him and shoved at one of the bodies with his foot. "These guys are pretty well preserved. They don't appear to be decomposed much at all. Ugh!" The arm he had just pushed snapped off at the shoulder, nearly sending him tumbling into the pile. "It's like they were frozen. There are no signs of wounds or blood that I can see."

"Poor bastards probably starved to death." Frank had joined them and was scanning the bodies with his flashlight beam. "What's that?" he asked as the light reflected off something in the pile.

By now, Paulie's curiosity had gotten the better of him and he was getting up close and personal, shining his tactical light at a couple of the bodies. "You guys got a problem with somebody messin' with dead people?"

"Well, I think if it was our guys..." Max started nobly, trying to get a better look at the source of the reflected light.

Paulie finished his thought, "But these guys ain't even from this time or place from the looks of 'em. So all's fair, right?"

He bent down to take hold of the sandaled feet of one of the corpses and dragged it from the pile. Now separated from the group, it became clear that the dead were outfitted in strange clothes and some were armed with small hand weapons.

"Is that Roman gear? I've been to museums and seen a ton of movies, but I've never seen armor like this." Charles was examining the golden plates that clung tightly to the chest of the corpse. He pulled at it and was surprised to find that it seemed to be held together by some type of cloth mesh that stretched like elastic.

"Whoa, check this shit out!" He pulled a metal plate away from the armor and let it go. It snapped back and made a 'twang' as it fit back into the rest of the armor. "And it's like someone alive is wearing it! It's still warm!"

"Holy shit! Did you see that?" Frank sounded very excited. "This can't be real."

"What are you talking about, boss?" Archer stepped closer to one of the corpses and repeated what Charles had done. "I see what you mean. This shouldn't be…"

"What are you guys sayin?" Max stooped down to get a better look.

Frank had a strange look of wonder. "It's like elastic, except I'm guessing elastic hadn't been invented when these guys were alive. Anyway, it should have broken down and rotted with the bodies." The gears of his imagination were already turning. He had an idea.

"See that thing over there? What is that?" he said, pointing at a dull shine coming from under one of the stiffs. "Can you grab it, Max?"

Max stepped gingerly through the mass of bodies, carefully placing each foot so as not to step on any part of one. It less from respect than fear that he would lose his balance and fall down on top of one of them.

"What do you think killed these guys, Frank?" He bent over to move an arm with the base of his flashlight, and there it was – a short, silver sword. He quickly snatched it up and retraced his steps back to the open floor area.

In the relative security of the team, he examined the sword in the beam of his light. "You gotta check this out!"

Everyone gathered around Max as he turned the sword in his hand to get a look at the other side.

"That is a fine piece," Frank admired the sword. "It looks like people carved into the blade."

"Yeah man," Paulie replied. "and they look more like skeletons. It's like they're crawling on their knees down to the tip of the blade. What do you think that red stone is? Is it a ruby?"

"Hard to say if it's an actual gem stone in this dim light. If it is, it's not cut like one. It's just kind of mounted there in the center of the shaft." Max held the blade out.

Frank stepped up now and took it from Max to examine it closer. "I don't think this is made for battle. It maybe more a decorative piece, or ceremonial sword, I would think. The way the stone is mounted on the blade so close to the grip would weaken its striking capability."

"Well, whatever it is, the thing is fuckin' creepy," Charles offered.

Suddenly, it dawned on Frank that Paulie was right in the thick of the conversation. "Aren't you supposed to be keeping guard on our friend over there?"

"Yeah, but he wasn't interested in girl talk, so I came over here to see what was goin' on." He was grinning as usual until he looked over at the vacant area where the statue had been. "Oh shit! It's gone!"

"Ready your weapons! That thing is somewhere in here. We need to get out of this hole right now." Frank ordered his men, "Everybody to the rope, let's go! Yank on it three times. They're waiting to pull you up."

First to the rope was Charles. He wasted no time climbing up toward the gaping hole above them as the men above pulled him upward. He had tied the bag of gold to his belt, and with each advance, it swung out behind him. Just as he was pulled up and out, he could hear the roar behind him. The sound was blood curdling like the roar of a lion combined with the call of an elephant. He was glad when his feet hit the road.

"Throw some more ropes down. We need to get the guys out NOW!" He yelled as he ran toward the truck.

"What's going on?" Clark hollered as they searched the Humvee for another rope.

"There's a giant fucking four-armed Cyclops down there, and I think he's pissed!" Charles responded.

Underground, Frank had retrieved a carry bag from the fallen Humvee and shoved as many of the scrolls as he could fit into it. As he headed toward the ropes, the monster suddenly made its appearance. It was coming at them from the other end of the chamber, and by the sound of its roar, there was no doubting its intentions.

"Fire some warning shots!" thundered Frank. "Try to slow it down to give us more time."

Paulie and Archer sprayed the ground with lead in front of the approaching terror, but it didn't even flinch as the bullets pummeled the ground at its feet. It just kept coming.

"Fuck this!" yelled Paulie, and leveled his weapon at its legs. "This should slow him down."

The spray would have blown the legs off an ordinary man, but the Cyclops just roared again and kept coming. The bullets either passed straight through him or were absorbed by his soft flesh. Max slid the sword into his belt and was climbing up the rope when the creature made for him.

Paulie ran in the opposite direction, trying to distract. "Hey, you big ugly motherfucker! Your mom just called and…" He fired his pistol at the center of the Cyclops' hairless chest as he spoke. "She lied when she told you that you were the mailman's kid. Your daddy's a fuckin' pit bull!"

He fired more rounds and watched as they penetrated its skin leaving holes that closed immediately after impact. The last thing that Paulie wanted was to get caught. The creature was definitely faster than he was, so he turned and ran for his life.

When the beast caught up to him, it reached out to grab him with its two right arms. One hand successfully closed on the back of his jacket. Paulie yelled, "Shit!" as the Cyclops lifted him easily and threw him across the chamber like an angry child tossing its doll. Frank and the others waiting to climb out watched helplessly as Paulie landed in a crumpled pile on the floor. It was hard to tell if he were alive or dead.

Max reached the surface and was crawling over the edge when he heard Paulie yell. He had no idea what was going on behind him, but he was glad to see the guys tossing two more ropes into the chamber below. "Hurry and get them out of there. There's some kind of fuckin' monster tearing them apart!"

Clark and the others had been feeding the ropes out from coils, but now they tossed the piles of loops into the hole. "Grab on! We'll pull you up." Clark yelled into the hole.

Frank needed to get to Paulie somehow, but the creature was standing directly between them and pounding its chest like an ape. He would try provoking a chase, and then he would be the one to deal with it. He needed to get everyone out of there in one piece. From the left he could see Malcolm and Archer climbing up the ropes. Now only Paulie and he remained. He had to think fast.

"Hey, over here, you piece of shit!"

Trotting backward away from Paulie, Frank moved toward the bodies along the wall. As he ran, he pulled two grenades from his belt. The thing was far enough from Paulie now to limit any risk to him from the explosions, so Frank grasped the pins on both grenades and pulled them.

"Paulie, if you can hear me, man, stay down and cover your ears," he yelled as he threw the grenades at the enraged beast. He dropped to the ground covering his ears and watched as the Cyclops caught the grenades.

"Nice catch!" he yelled at his target.

The beast stood examining the curious items in his hands. Suddenly, two bright flashes and a very loud, *Boom! Boom!* Blown to pieces, bloody chunks of the creature sprayed around the chamber and its body fluids misted over the men.

Slowly Frank got to his knees, and stood calling out to Paulie, "Paulie, you all right?"

He was relieved to hear, "Yeah, I think so. Just give me a second to get my shit together."

Frank walked toward the bruised soldier. Smiling, he called, "You in a hurry to get out of here, or do you have a minute to take one more look around?"

Paulie was incredulous. He shook his head. "Right. Sure, I guess I owe ya."

Frank offered his hand and Paulie grasped it pulling himself up. As he was rising, he noticed something strange on Frank's arm. "What the fuck?"

It was then that Frank felt something strange. He looked to see what was moving on his arm. Several chunks of filthy Cyclops flesh had rained down on him in the explosion, and now those chunks were twitching as though they had a life of their own. Suddenly, they were flying off in the direction of the rest of remains of the beast. As their eyes followed the trajectory, they saw something that made Frank gasp.

"Fuck me!"

Across the chamber, even in the dim light, they could see bits of flesh flying from all directions and slamming together to form the large clump of roiling flesh now beginning to take shape on the floor.

"Let's go! Run, Paulie!" Frank yelled as he pulled the injured man. He was half dragging him toward the two ropes left dangling from the ground above. They were about fifteen feet away when Frank began to hear a gurgling, growling sound behind them.

At the rope, Frank helped Paulie tie it around his waist and hollered, "Hold on, man." Tugging on the rope, he called up to anyone who could hear him, "Pull him up!"

On the surface, the men got the signal and pulled Paulie like a shot toward the surface. Frank watched him reach the rim of the hole and bump out into the sunlight while he tied the last rope around himself. He gave it a couple of tugs and grabbed the bag containing the scrolls as he braced himself for the jerk of the rope from above.

Nothing happened.

Behind him, the sound of a large growling dog was coming very close. He did not want to look back, but he couldn't help himself. He had to see what was coming to get him.

It appeared to be a gigantic two-headed dog dripping with drool, the edges of its lips curled up. Frank was terrified to see canine teeth as big as he could ever imagine. Crouching, the beast was in position to jump. Thankfully, he still had his pistol tucked in his belt. As he pulled it out and started firing shot after shot into the thing, he suddenly rocketed toward the surface. The dog from hell was leaping up at him. Its jaws were snapping, missing his feet by inches.

Seconds before he cleared the rim, he saw the monster turning to make another attempt. In an instant, he was up and out into the blinding sunlight, being pulled along the surface of the road. As he slid to a stop, he yelled out, "Blow it! Use a big charge! It's coming up…"

Just as the words escaped his lips, the two-headed dog cleared the hole and landed nearly three yards from his feet. It was smooth and hairless, like the Cyclops from which it had been formed. Its heads were twisting as it began to shake. Looking skyward with both heads, it let loose an unearthly howl as Frank scrambled away sideways like a crab. Everyone was retreating, but the creature did not advance.

The men readied their weapons and prepared to open fire. The beast's skin began to crack, the damage spreading quickly as it stood motionless. Then, with the sound of thunder, it exploded into dust.

"What the fuck was that?" Joe asked, still holding the fifty cal he had readied for the kill. "I never even got off a shot!"

"Really not sure," Frank replied, getting up from the ground and brushing the dust from his clothes. "But I can say one thing, I fucking hate dogs!"

Thirty-Six

"So you're saying there is a chance we are gonna run into something like that when we go through there?" Emily nodded toward the darkened shape on the sandstone wall.

"Uh, well, there's more." Paulie slid his chair back from behind the computer. "Frank told me that when he finally found someone who could translate those scrolls, not only did he end up with the plans for this machine," he waved his hand toward the strange contraption, "but there was some stuff there about what's on the other side."

"The other side?" John was checking out the wall. "What kind of stuff?"

"You've heard of purgatory?" Malcolm asked.

"Yeah, Catholics say it's a place somewhere between heaven and hell, right? Spirits get stuck there or something, like a waiting room at a hospital or something." Emily couldn't believe they were having a conversation about religion at a time like this.

"You're kinda right, but this place is more like hell from what Frank said."

"Okay, so what does that mean?" Emily was growing impatient with all the mystery. "How 'bout we just get to the point or get going?"

"Have you ever seen the video game, *Dominion of Broken Souls?* Well, that was one of our games. I did the character design for that one." Malcolm was staring down at the floor and his voice growing lower as he spoke. "I designed the characters in that world from descriptions contained in those scrolls."

"What?" This bit of information was upsetting to Clark. "The creatures in that game were truly fucking terrifying! Especially that thing that attaches itself to your back and sucks out your life force."

"Okay, okay, enough of the chatter. There's only one thing to decide here." John stepped into the center of the group and turned around looking at each one as he spoke. "Are you going or not? No one will blame you if you stay back here with Paulie. I owe Frank for all he has done for Emily and me. I can't say we'd be alive today if he hadn't come for us up in those woods."

"I'm in." Max stepped forward. "I doubt that anyone here is gonna sit this out."

"He's right. I think between Baghdad and San Fran, there probably ain't nobody saved as many asses as Frank." Joe was finally speaking out. "And, brother, there's a good group of 'em here today. Let's get this party started."

The others were nodding as John looked around. "Em, are you sure you're up for this?"

"I don't have a choice, John. You think I'm gonna let you go in there while I stand here wondering what's happening to you? No way. We're partners in more ways than one." She smiled and gave him a playful shove.

"Right then. So let's go down to the armory and gear up."

He walked out of the door and across the hall to press his hand against the painting. In a moment, the elevator was exposed.

"Good morning, John." The pleasant voice cooed at him through the speakers of the elevator as the doors opened, "Late visit to the armory today."

"We're going after Frank, Alice," he replied. "He's in trouble."

"You must hurry. They are coming for him." The voice was soothing, so soothing in fact that John missed the warning at first.

"Who's coming?" Joe demanded, frustrated with John's hesitation.

"In the darkness, they feed on their souls," the voice responded flatly. "Safe hunting, John."

"What the fuck was that?" Max asked, examining the speaker fixture in the wall. "They're coming for him? Fuckin' feed on their souls?"

"Easy, Max. It's probably a warning from somewhere beyond. We've heard this kind of thing before." Emily leaned against John, her head resting gently on his shoulder.

"So what did it mean? When you heard it before?" Max had a near crazed look in his eyes.

"Wherever Frank is, it sounds like there's something there that takes or destroys people's souls." She sounded all too casual.

"So how are we supposed to process that fucked up tidbit of information?" asked Clark.

"You don't process it, Clark. You find it and kill it, or you avoid it and survive. What other option is there?" She sighed.

"John, how do you ever get any sleep lying next to such a gorgeous badass of a woman?" Joe asked with a smile.

John winked at Emily. "Usually about half erect and with one eye open."

Thirty-Seven

Once in the armory, John tried to determine the best mix of weapons to take based on the Archer's story. "Hey, you guys said bullets didn't faze the Cyclops, right?" The others were standing in front of the rack of fully automatic weapons.

Archer stepped forward. "Right. Although the light was pretty poor, and it was hard to see from where I stood, Frank and Paulie have told us that the bullets had little if any effect."

Paulie agreed. "They either passed right through the beast or were somehow absorbed."

"Did it slow the monster down at least?" Emily was fingering a pistol lying on the counter in front of her.

"I guess you could say so, but the explosives worked best. To me, the craziest thing about it was when it blew to pieces and somehow, instead of dying, it came flying back together and turned into a two-headed dog. That's some crazy shit if you ask me." Paulie was shaking his head.

"Yeah, the whole thing sounds crazy." Everyone was nodding as John tried to get back on point. "So, we only want to take weapons that we know are effective. No point in loading ourselves down with a hundred pounds of iron and lead if it has no more effect than a mosquito."

He was rubbing his jaw. "Then again, it's possible there are other beings there that can be killed with bullets. I don't know what to tell you, just get whatever you think you'll need."

"Hey, Arch," Emily called out to Archer as he turned back to choose his weapons. "When you were telling the story… you know the part when the dog jumped out into the sunlight? You said it cracked up and turned to dust, right?"

"Yeah, but…"

"I have an idea." John walked toward the other guys. "Have any of you seen flashlights or scope lights?"

"Yeah, there's a cabinet back over there, says *Lights* in big black letters right in front of it." Joe pointed the way.

John was already moving toward it. "I'm thinking there was something about the sunlight that killed that thing. I'm thinking maybe a particular spectrum of light – infrared or ultraviolet, maybe."

"Can you, uh… explain that, Mr. Wizard?" Joe knew a lot about a lot of things, but did not have much real education.

"You've seen black lights at those strip clubs you like to go to, I'm guessing." Emily tried to put it into terms that Joe could understand.

"Oh yeah. It makes the girls look like they have a really nice tan."

"Well, those are actually ultraviolet lights. When I was a detective, we used them to look for traces of blood or semen," John added.

"I coulda used that with my ex-wife!" Phillip's sudden outburst came as a surprise to the group. "I swear that bitch fucked every pool boy and personal trainer from here to…"

"Anyway…" John interrupted him, holding his hand out to indicate that Philip should probably hold that thought. "Infrared lights that you can carry around are rare, but I bet Frank has some ultra…"

Digging in one of the cabinets, he pulled out three boxed handheld fluorescent lamps. "Speak of the devil. Exactly the kind we used on the force. These babies are powerful." He handed them to Emily who added them to the smaller bag she was carrying. John distributed the rest to the others.

"Hey, check this shit!" Clark yelled from across the room. In a moment, he appeared from around a corner brandishing three swords. "Arch, isn't this your sword from the story?"

Archer took one of the swords Clark was holding and turned it over. "That is definitely it, but I thought we only brought back one."

"You guys know how Frank is," Paulie said. "Gotta have at least three of everything. I think he commissioned some Japanese sword maker to do the copies. We needed them for the games, but Frank insisted that they were identical to the original. Said we might need 'em someday, and here we are!"

"This is some amazing shit," John observed, checking out the swords for himself. "I can't even tell which one is the original."

"Is there anything Frank doesn't have?" Paulie wasn't jealous. Frank had worked hard for what he had, and Paulie admired him. "I mean, this armory, this house – he has everything!"

"Except a girlfriend." Emily threw out. "Maybe, if we find him, we can hook him up with one."

"I'm sure he wants our help with that," one of the guys answered.

"Maybe he would. Have any of you ever asked him if he's lonely?"

They all shook their heads.

"No, there are some things we just don't talk about. I tried to hook him up with a friend once," said Joe.

"And what did he say?"

Joe smiled, "He said, *'Relationships are like sports cars... you drive carefully until you feel comfortable, but sooner or later even the most experienced driver is gonna crash and burn. I might be rich, but I can't afford the insurance.'* Never asked him again."

"What the hell is that supposed to mean?" Emily asked.

"I figured it was some fancy kind of way to tell me to fuck off, so I didn't ask him to explain."

Archer had been examining the swords during the exchange, but now he interrupted, "I figured it out. This one is the real sword. If you look close, you can see it has some scratches, the other two are way too clean to be old."

"Bring it, Archer. Is everyone else good to go?" John shouted across the room.

A hearty "Oorah!" came the reply.

"Alright then, let's get this carnival on the road!" With that, he headed toward the door.

"John, it's almost sunrise. Can we take a minute before we go? It might be our last." Emily was suddenly somber.

"Sure, wild thing." He put his arm around her. "Anything for you."

As they stepped into the elevator, each of them loaded down with gear, she mumbled almost to herself, "If it was anything I wanted, we wouldn't be doing this because Frank wouldn't have disappeared."

"What was that?" John asked.

"I said, 'This is one adventure I wouldn't want to miss,'" she said, forcing a smile as she eyed the guys standing before her. She felt a bit ashamed knowing that they were all there willing to risk their lives for their friend. "God help us!"

"God help us indeed!" agreed Max.

Thirty-Eight

John and Emily stood together on the wide front steps, the entry to Frank's giant fortress of a home. The sun was just beginning to dip below the hills in the distance. A beautiful orange sky painted with bands of purple clouds made for one of the most stunning sunrises Emily had ever seen.

"What do you think it is gonna be like there, John?" She looked into his eyes and took his hand.

"Judging by the story Arch told, it could be hell. At the very least, it will be strange. After all, he didn't say anything about how the scrolls might have gotten there or where the Cyclops came from, just that we were most likely in for some weird shit."

"So if anything happens…"

He cut her off, "I'm not saying nothing's gonna happen," he pulled her tighter to him, "but with every breath and beat of my heart, I promise I will not let anything happen to you, baby."

"I know I have been snarky lately with all the stuff that's happened and getting the business started." Emily looked up at him and at the expression on his face. "This paranormal stuff, well, it takes some adjustment. You know? It's not just some weird show on TV."

She squeezed his hand. "I want to tell you before we go in there that I've never felt the way I feel about you… before, with anyone, so we gotta come out of this in one piece." With a chuckle, she added, "or at least in good enough shape that we can still…"

Now she choked up. "I know we owe it to Frank to do this, so I guess we better get going. The guys are waiting for us."

"Right, and Emily…" He pushed the words out as his heart skipped a beat, "Don't ever doubt how much I love you."

"I know, John, I know." Squeezing his hand, she quickly wiped the moisture from her eye before it had a chance to spill over and run down her cheek.

Thirty-Nine

The conversation coming from the computer lab was peppered with laughter. Everyone was gathered there, armed and ready. As John and Emily entered the room, John cleared his throat. "All right, let's do this. We're gonna toss that chair through first and make sure we can get it back. After that, we'll need a volunteer to go through and test for air."

"I got that," said Joe stepping forward. "What else should I look for while I'm there?"

"Regular recon, Joe, lay of the land and all. I know you're good at holding your breath, but the second you step through, if there's no air, jump right back through. Hopefully, there won't be any trouble getting back. I have to say it, if there's no air, or the conditions are too extreme, then there's a good chance that Frank is dead already. If that's how it is, then our plan is toast. Got me, guys?"

"We got you, sir." They spoke in near unison.

"Max, go ahead and get a rope on that chair. Everyone else, grab the loose end." John was pointing as he spoke. "Paulie, fire that thing up, and let's see what we've got."

"Alright, John, but I can only keep it open for about five or ten minutes, so we gotta do this quick."

"We're ready. Let's do it."

Paulie sat down at the keyboard and typed furiously, his fingers flying over the keyboard. Emily marveled that someone as coarse as Paulie could be so tech savvy. As suddenly as he had begun to type, he stopped. His hand hovered above the keyboard with his index finger extended.

"Here we go!" With that, he pressed the Enter key.

The machine let out a low-pitched hum, its pitch becoming higher as the hum grew louder. The large crystals began to vibrate as John and the others watched, wide-eyed and ready. As the crystals began to glow, faint beams of violet colored light shone upon the wall. The team watched as a thousand pinpoints of light danced across the sandstone, and then, all at once… it was gone.

Before them the wall opened up as wide as an average garage door, and tall enough for them to walk through without bending.

"The chair, throw it!" John yelled.

Joe stood holding the chair at the front of the group. He pulled it back and swung wide. As he stepped up to release it, he was hit with the stench of foul air. The bile rose in his throat while the others coughed and gagged. The room was filled with the smell of death. Emily covered her face with her arm in an attempt to block the smell. Her eyes began to water.

The chair had flown through the portal, and the slack of the rope lay limp on the floor. When it went taut and began to jerk in the hands of those holding on to it, John counted to ten in his head before choking out the words, "Pull it back!"

The team reacted quickly, pulling on the rope until the chair slid back inside the room, dusty and scratched up but no worse for wear. Joe took hold of it to see whether it had changed temperature only to discover that there had been no change. He looked behind him over his shoulder, first nodding at John and Emily, then at the rest. Winking, he opened his mouth and sucked in as much air as he could. With a smile, he turned to the portal and charged through.

"Not yet, Joe!" John yelled, but he was already gone.

In less than a minute, he was running back into the room. He was a bit winded, but other than the dust on his shoes, he was otherwise unscathed.

"Shut it down!" yelled John as he rushed toward Joe.

Paulie hit the ESC key and the machine wound down, the wall closing up behind Joe. John reached out to steady him. "Whatcha got, soldier? You straight?"

"Holy shit, I was lost! I nearly didn't find my way back." Joe was out of breath.

"You weren't even in there for a minute, Joe. How could you get lost?" Archer didn't have to look at his watch. It seemed no sooner had Joe stepped out than he was back.

"Well, to me it seemed like half an hour at least," Joe huffed. "I need to sit down." He looked exhausted.

"Chair." Max pushed the dusty chair behind Joe forcing him to sit.

Charles wanted to get to the point. "So tell us, what's over there?" The others gathered around.

"I really felt lost. The sky there has a red glow to it, like some really wild sunset. I tried to locate something to navigate by, but I didn't see any sun."

"It's okay, Joe. Take a second to gather your thoughts," said Emily, hoping to get him to focus. "What else did you see?"

"I gotta tell ya, that hole doesn't look the same from the other side. In fact, over there, it opens into some kind of field. That's where the dust came from. I ran about a hundred yards in a sweep and then, and when I was ready to come back, I couldn't see the portal at all. It had moved. I had to run, searching to find it. When we go, we need to mark our trail somehow so we can find our way back."

"Like Hansel and Gretel?" John smiled at him, patting his shoulder.

"Yeah, I guess. We could take a long rope…."

"Nah, rope won't work," Clark interrupted. "What if we need more distance than we can get with any rope? How about notching trees? Were there trees, Joe?"

"No, man. Like I said, it was a field. An open field. I can't even say it was a grassy field. There ain't no real trees or grass where I was."

"What about paint? I think Frank has spray cans of primer in the garage," John suggested.

Malcolm blurted out, "You need spray cans? I'll be right back," and left the room.

"What the fuck?" John didn't know whether to be more irked or perplexed by Malcolm's sudden exit.

"Mal's a tagger," Phillip told him. "I think he went to get something out of his car."

"A tagger?" Emily hadn't heard the term before.

"He does graffiti. You've seen that bridge overpass that has the landscape painted on it with the naked lady?"

John was surprised. "He painted that? That's really hot!"

Emily elbowed him in the ribs. "I hope he has a can for everybody."

Forty

While the team waited for Malcolm to return from his car, John handed Joe a bottle of water from his backpack. "So, you said the portal doesn't look the same from the other side. What does it look like, exactly?"

"I don't really know how to explain it other than…" He stopped to think for a moment. "You know what it's like when you're out in the country on a hot day, driving down a country road? You know how you look up ahead and the road looks like it's wet and shimmery, like little waves, but it's really dry?"

"You mean a mirage?" John suggested.

"Yeah like that, but I it's not really the wet look. There are shimmery ripples around the opening, but they're not really there. Like some kind of energy or something."

Just then, Malcolm returned carrying an old milk crate full of spray cans. "I grabbed all of the brightest colors. I got white, green, yellow, some fluorescents…"

"Good stuff, Mal. Everybody take a couple of cans," John instructed. "When we're over there, we need to mark our trail at least every fifty steps or so. Whoever's in the rear, it'll be your responsibility. We can rotate every hour or so to keep it fresh. If you run out of paint, let us know. I don't want to get left hanging over there."

He turned to Joe. "Anything else we need to know before we do this?"

"Well, there isn't a lot of light. Make sure we have lots of flashlights and flares…" He looked around the room as the guys were nodding and patting various packs and pouches in acknowledgement. "I heard a scream and some moaning, but I couldn't tell where it was coming from. There might have been a few trees here and there in the distance, but they looked like they didn't have leaves on them so maybe they weren't really trees. You gotta remember I was looking for the portal, not a place to have a picnic."

"Well, I guess that's all we got to go on for now. Everybody got paint, flares and flashlights?" The team nodded as John looked around. "Grenades and explosives?"

"Dude, I even got a couple of bricks of C4!" Archer beamed.

"Wow, Frank really does have something for any situation," Emily observed.

"Someone say the prayer before we go," Joe suggested.

"I've got this one," said Max, and the team gathered around him as he began. "Lord, we are humble before you as we begin this mission." Although it began with the usual language of prayer, the longer it went on the less usual it became. "…And though we may have to kill every damn thing in that place in order to come home safely we know it is your will for us to do so for you send no angel to do the Devil's work."

When finished, everyone shouted, "Oorah!" including John and Emily who were now thoroughly immersed in the spirit of camaraderie. Both understood why these guys did the things they did. It had become their mission in life, to watch out for one another.

"All right then! We go in two by two, so pick your partner. Malcolm, you bring up the rear, so get your paint can ready. We'll be waiting for you when you get there. Once we go through, try not to get too far outside the view of the group." Then he turned to Paulie, "Fire that motherfucker up! When it reaches the critical point, shut it down and let it cool off, then fire it up again at one hour intervals until we get back."

"Got it." Paulie nodded and wheeled his chair to the keyboard. He began typing furiously and once he hit the Enter key, the humming began.

The guys lined up ready to go, Joe and Archer in the lead. John and Emily were next in line with the rest of the team behind them. The pitch of the machine rose and the crystals began to vibrate. They stood to the side watching as the stone wall began to shimmer and the points of violet light began to shine.

John turned to Paulie, and yelled over the noise from the machine. "Leave this thing open as long as you can in case we need to turn right around!"

"You'll have about ten minutes. I can't promise more than that," Paulie shouted back.

"If anything tries to come through from the other side in the meantime, use Frank's gun and kill it." John lifted his weapon.

Paulie nodded. He was ready for anything. He had retrieved his own weapons cache from the armory.

John turned toward the portal and yelled, "Go, Go, Go!"

Forty-One

Joe and Archer headed through the opening just as a stiff wind blew the stench directly into their faces. It was undeniably the smell of death, free of modern perfumes and deodorizers. When it was her turn to step through, Emily held her nose, which made her ears pop like when the pressure changes on an airplane only ten times over.

"Ouch. What the hell?" Emily exclaimed as they jogged beyond the point of entry to allow the rest of the team to pass through behind them. "Joe didn't say anything about his ears popping!" She put her fingertip into her ear.

"I didn't expect it either," John said as he adjusted the band of his hat and put it back on his head.

Two by two, the rest of the team passed from one world into another. As each pair went through, the machine inside Frank's lab changed in pitch from it highest vibration to somewhere mid-range. It was as though they put a burden on the power load with each breach of the gateway.

As John looked around, he realized that he and Emily were alone. "Where is everybody?" He turned back to the portal to see who was coming through, but nothing was there but a dim and unfriendly landscape. "What happened?"

A few seconds later, he saw his answer running toward them. "We thought we lost you guys until Joe figured out which way the portal is moving. We've been running to try and catch it." Archer paused to catch his breath.

"I guess, when I was here before, I wasn't lost after all. The damn portal actually keeps on moving!"

"Does it move in a circle or a straight line?" John was still getting his bearings.

"I'm not sure," Joe answered. "All I know is that I ran around until I found it again and stepped through back to Frank's."

For a few minutes, they discussed how to proceed and where to look for the others. They needed to figure out how it would be possible to return once they were able to find Frank. They had no good ideas. From the opposite direction, they heard someone calling to them.

"Hey, guys, why didn't you wait for us?" It was Max and Phillip jogging toward them.

"How far did you guys come from the portal?" Based on the direction they had been running, John was starting to get his bearings on which way the portal was moving.

"About a quarter click that way." Max pointed behind his back.

Archer was bent over spraying a mark on the ground with one of the paint cans. "I marked where we came out before we saw you guys."

"Yeah, we did too, just in case," Max assured them.

"So, if you guys came out there," John said pointing, "and Phil and Max came out over there, where are the rest going to end up? The portal must be moving pretty fast."

"That makes sense. Like I said before, I had trouble finding my way out." Joe seemed almost relieved to know that he wasn't crazy. He took pride in his inner compass.

"Come on, let's get our asses to where the rest of the guys are gonna come through." John took off jogging in the direction from where Philip and Max had come and the rest of the team trailed behind him. He estimated the next two would emerge from the gateway several clicks ahead.

Moments later, they passed an X sprayed on the ground. They were definitely going the right way.

It was as Joe had related to them, a formidable landscape. There was light casting a reddish hue over everything in sight, but no real sun. The terrain was flat, like the plains of the Midwest, but without the tall grasses. The rolling hills and large mountains to either side of them rose up in stark contrast. Unlike mountain ranges at home, these had sharp jagged peaks that seemed to claw and scratch at the hazy sky. There was no recognizable plant life in the immediate area, but to the edge of the foothills, it looked as though some type of trees dotted the landscape.

"This place is some weird shit," Max huffed as they jogged along a line they hoped would lead to the rest of the team.

"Look over there! What the hell is that?" Emily pointed where a cluster of glowing spheres were drifting toward them. As the team focused in the direction her finger was pointing, they did not notice the shimmering portal right before them. From out of nowhere, Clark and Charles stepped into their path. By the time the group realized what had happened, they were already slamming into them.

"Shit!" John and Emily tumbled to the ground along with the new arrivals. A small cloud of dust rose to surround them. Those who had been trailing behind them were able to stop just before stomping their friends.

"Sorry guys." John pushed himself up and held out his hand to help Emily. Then he offered a hand to help Charles. "What Joe couldn't tell us earlier was the fact that the portal keeps moving. So we've been chasing it this way hoping to find you."

"How much do you fuckin' weigh, John?" Charles said dusting himself off. "Felt like a damn bus hit me!"

Clark was on his knees gathering up items that had been discharged from his pack on impact. "Play football much, Emily? You've got one hell of a blocking technique." He didn't notice that, less than a foot away, the ground had begun to churn. He motioned with his head to Archer. "Give me a hand here, Arch. Help me pick this shit up."

His friend seemed to be absorbed by the strange sight behind him. Coming their way were about a dozen glowing orbs. As Clark turned his head to see what everyone was looking at, four thin snake-like tentacles shot out of the ground and wrapped around his wrist and hand.

"What the… AWW… that fucking hurts!" he cried out as the tentacles tightened around his wrist and began jerking him toward the ground. Struggling to pull himself free, he began to panic when the first foul finger broke through his skin. "Help me!" he shrieked. "Get this thing off me!"

The fear welled up in his eyes as he lost his balance and was pulled face-first to the ground. Whatever had a hold on him was not about to release its prize. More tentacles shot from the ground to grip his forearm just below the elbow.

The others were now aware that something terrible was happening, but from where they were standing, they could not see what it was. Clark's body was blocking their view, and in the seconds it took them to react, his arm was nearly covered with tentacles. Several of them had already burrowed into his skin. At the sound of Clark's spine-chilling scream, whatever it was that had taken hold of him decided to flee.

All at once Clark was dragged along the ground by his infested arm. The tentacles broke up the ground like a buried electrical cord being yanked free. He flipped and flopped as the dirt gave way ahead of him and flew back into his face. He choked as chunks of dirt flew into his screaming mouth as the others ran after him.

Although John led the charge, it was Emily who dove for Clark's feet while he was being dragged away. She hit the ground with a hard thud, her hands barely missing his foot as he shot away. "Shit! Grab him!" she yelled as she got back to her feet.

John was scrambling in the lead and was finally able to grab on to Clark's boot and pull. "Help me!" he shouted at the others as he struggled for a better grip. For the moment, he was sure they would be able to halt Clark's abduction.

Clark was resisting with all of his might. He struggled to reach the knife on his belt, thinking he could cut himself loose. Just as the tips of his fingers located the knife, several new tentacles shot up from the ground. Longer than the first, they slapped against his face as they struck out at him. He tried using his free arm to knock them away lest his head become entangled.

Now the crew had him by both legs, two to a leg but the creature was still managing to pull them along. The tentacles that had originally attacked him were now embedded firmly in the muscles of his forearm. The guys holding on to his legs attempted to encourage him, shouting, "We got you, man, hang on!" but their confidence was beginning to fade.

For a brief moment, Clark clung to the hope that the others would be able to save him. However, the terrible creature, which had been dragging all of them along on the cracked and dusty ground, finally revealed itself. With a loud bellow, it came up from the depths, the dirt rolling off its back as its massive multi-legged body was exposed.

"Holy shit! What the fuck is that?" yelled Max as adrenalin screamed through his body. The monster was nearly ten feet in diameter and looked like a gigantic spider with a huge spherical body. Two eyes protruded on short stalks from its relatively tiny head. They were directed at the intruders, and now that it could see them, it tried even harder to pull them closer.

A large split appeared down its side as it opened its jaws. Its mouth opened wide enough to swallow a man whole. Clark twisted and turned, screaming in horror. He was about to become a meal to the horrible alien creature. Warmth spread through his jeans as he pissed himself.

John was not ready to give up. "Everybody dig your feet in! Nobody's going out like this on my watch." He shifted his stance to give his feet better traction. As the others followed his lead, suddenly Clark was suspended mid-air in a vicious tug of war. On one side was a creature more terrifying than any monster he had ever conjured up in his worst nightmares. On the other side, his friends were desperately trying to save him.

With the monster fully exposed, Max raised his weapon. He stepped to the side to protect his friends and fired on the massive creature. Round after round found its mark. He should have been rewarded by the creature's screaming death, but its flesh simply absorbed the lead. The wounds sealed over as if nothing had happened.

Emily watched in horror as the bullets had no more effect than a gnat hitting a window screen. She felt helpless to do anything to help until she saw a glint of light from something sticking out of Archer's backpack. It was the sword they had brought back from Iraq.

"Archer, the sword! Use the sword," she yelled at him, but the sounds of Clark's screams and the roars of the beast drowned out the sound of her voice. Without a word, she went for it, yanking the blade from its lashings.

She was shaking as she moved into position in front of the men. They were losing their footing and the battle for

Clark's life. At any moment, they might lose their grip on him, sending him tumbling into the snapping jaws of his captor. She caught her breath as she brought the sword back for a chopping swing. The look of terror and pain in Clark's eyes was all she needed to overcome her fear as she aimed for the monstrous tentacles.

As she brought the weapon down, the tentacles suddenly snapped. The men tried to steady themselves as the tension abruptly released, but they nearly tripped over one another as they tried to regain their balance. The severed appendages flailed on the ground, spewing a dark green fluid.

"Emily! Toss me the…" John yelled. "Awww! Fuck this!" He reached for a grenade on his belt as the others scrambled to pull Clark clear. The monster howled in agony and rage. It seemed acutely aware that its meal was escaping. Ripping the remaining length of its legs out of the ground, it leaned to one side as it moved awkwardly toward the men. Its jaws were open wide and snapping as it came.

"Eat this you ugly fucker!" John pulled the pin from the grenade and tossed it into the huge chomping mouth. The monster's jaws snapped shut. The team tightened their hold on Clark and began to run in the opposite direction, dragging him along. They got as far away from the beast as possible before the grenade went off with a loud WHOOMP! Gore flew in all directions, spraying the brownish-green blood and bits of flesh onto the backs of the fleeing men.

Clark lay on the ground soaked in his own piss and crying out as the tentacles, still embedded in his arm, pulsed with life and continued growing.

"Those fucking things are eating him alive!" Max yelled. "We gotta do something!"

The rush of the rescue was still dissipating, and no one had a clear head. Anyone touching the tentacles would surely be at risk to have the things become embedded in their own flesh. As they considered what to do, the scattered remains of the creature began to twitch with a life of their own. No one noticed as pieces of the monster began moving toward its exploded stump of a body.

"Hold him down. Get his belt off…" John yelled while Clark continued to writhe in pain.

They were soldiers. Though confused, they responded to John's command. Holding Clark down, they allowed his infested and swelling arm free to flail against the ground. John snatched the sword from Emily. She stood wild-eyed in shock, watching the scene unfold before her. He held the blade up waiting for his opportunity. The instant the arm stopped thrashing, he brought the blade down, lopping off Clark's arm above the elbow.

"Get that belt on him!" John dropped the sword and pushed down on Clark's shoulders while Max scrambled to get the belt around the gushing stump. Mercifully, Clark passed out cold.

Nearby, the severed limb lay motionless. The tentacles continued steadily pulsing until suddenly, they uncoiled. Quivering just above the arm, they hovered there momentarily before digging into the ground below and lifting the arm. The last they saw of it, the garish abomination was waving at them as it darted off toward the remains of the creature.

John watched as it wobbled away and couldn't believe his eyes as he noticed that other smaller bits of gore were airborne and returning to what was left of the monster's body. Finally, he realized what was happening. The beast was regenerating and not far from them.

"Fuck! That thing is putting itself back together! Joe, can you carry Clark?"

Joe turned to see the monster forming and didn't hesitate. "No problem."

"Get him over your shoulder then. We need to catch the portal!"

With a little help from Archer, Joe scooped up Clark who was still unconscious, and threw him over his shoulder. He straightened up and nodded at John. "Let's go."

Immediately, the group broke into a sprint to locate the portal. "When we catch up to portal, we need to wait to see if anyone is stepping through before we toss Clark back to the lab. Otherwise they could slam into each other," John called out between breaths. "Paulie can call for help before Clark bleeds out. We can't do shit to help him here."

Emily was running beside John and keeping pace, though she had to push herself to match his long strides.

Archer ran up beside them and shouted, "That was some quick thinking, girl. I thought we were gonna lose Clark for sure." He tried to glance over at her and nearly tripped at a dip in the terrain.

"It was a lucky shot," she panted.

"Clark owes you his ass, for sure."

Emily brushed back the lock of hair that had blown across her face. "I'm sure you would have done the same."

She was interrupted by someone behind her. "Hey, did you guys notice the spheres are following us?" There was a hint of panic in Max's voice. "They move when we move, and I think they are pacing us."

Emily was about to remind him that they had seen these before, when suddenly several yards ahead of them, Malcolm stepped from the portal.

"Get ready Joe!" John yelled over his shoulder. Joe was doing a heroic job of keeping up in spite of the weight of Clark over his shoulder.

Malcolm was still adjusting to the change and the discomfort in his ears. He turned to see where the voices were coming from.

John instructed the rest of the group to keep moving. He and Joe would get Clark to the portal, take care of business, and return to the group. He figured it could be difficult to get Clark through while the opening was moving so he did his best to get alongside of Joe. They could see the portal shimmering ahead of them.

"Get ready, Joe. We'll get in front of it and toss him through as it passes."

They had no idea whether Clark was conscious but John spoke to him anyway. "When you get through there, Clark, buddy, don't waste time telling stories. Call an ambulance first. Then you can shoot the shit all you want."

John and Joe positioned themselves well ahead of the moving portal. "This is good. Let's set him down." John slowed to a stop and faced Joe. "I'll get his shoulders, you grab his feet."

John lifted Clark under his armpits, and for the first time since Joe had picked him up, they heard him groan.

"On three! One…" They swung him once. "Two…" They swung him again, and the portal was nearly there. "Three!" As the portal passed, they tossed the injured man directly through its center. In an instant, Clark disappeared and the portal continued on its wide arc.

Forty-Two

Paulie never dreamt that something like this could actually exist. Yet, here it was, a portal to another world and his friends were stepping through it, two by two. Disappearing into where? He felt a twinge of jealousy as he tried to fill in the blanks of his imagination.

Malcolm was the last one through. Now he would wait about seven minutes before shutting the machine down. According to his calculations, if he let it cool down, he could repeat the process about every half hour. He turned back to check the computer screen when he heard a strange sound behind him. Twisting his chair around, he was amazed to see Clark flying through the portal and landing on the floor with a thud.

"Uhhhhhh." Clark was moaning, barely conscious, and bleeding badly in spite of the tourniquet wrapped around the stump of his arm.

"Oh shit!" Paulie nearly fell out of his chair to get to him. Kneeling beside him, he tried to get him to speak. "Dude, what the hell happened? You were only over there for about ten seconds!"

He pulled his phone out of his pocket and dialed 911. There was no sound. Paulie looked at the display and saw that there was no signal. He shoved the phone back in his pocket and helped Clark up from the floor. "Hang in there man. I'm going to get you some help."

He dragged Clark through the door and down the hall to the dining room where he quickly grabbed a chair and helped Clark slump down onto it. Blood dripped from his severed arm and onto the floor as Paulie ran to the door and tried the phone again. It rang twice before, "911, what's your emergency?"

"My friend... shit! Can you tell from my phone where I am? I don't know the address."

"Sir, I'm showing you at 101 DeMint Drive. What's your emergency?"

"My friend's arm has been torn off!"

"Hold please."

Paulie continued talking to Clark, trying to keep him calm.

"Sir? Emergency services have been dispatched. They should be at your location in approximately five minutes. Is your friend conscious? Can you identify the injured?"

"His name is Clark Ingram. He's in bad shape. Can you hurry? He's bleeding bad and barely conscious!"

"Don't worry, sir. We have him on file." He heard the thump – thump - thump of what sounded like a helicopter. "Life flight is landing at your location."

"That was fast!"

"Yes, sir. The paramedics are coming to the front door. Please unlock the door and lead them to the Mr. Ingram."

He turned off the phone and threw it aside. "Looks like you picked a good place to be in the shit, buddy. These guys are on it!"

He bent over Clark and eased him up over his shoulder. "They're gonna get you fixed up, no problem."

Paulie ran to the front door, warm blood dripping onto his shirt. "I gotta tell you, Clark... I love ya like a brother, but you're gonna owe me for the dry cleaning."

When he opened the door, the paramedics were already there. They took Clark from Paulie and laid him on a stretcher, setting up the IV they had brought with them and carrying him to the waiting chopper.

Forty-Three

John and Joe were covered in blood and sweat. Breathing hard, Joe was especially tired after the long run with Clark on his shoulder. They paused briefly to allow him to catch his breath before jogging to catch up with the rest of the team. They did not notice the spheres floating nearby.

Ahead of them, Archer was pointing over his shoulder. "Those spheres are still following us. What do you think they are?" No one had paid them much attention with all of the excitement.

Emily kept walking. "Who knows, after the monster we just killed, it could be just about any damn thing."

"Dude, I really don't want to find out what they are," Max declared as he stumbled into a rock on the ground ahead of him. "Oh shit!" he yelled as the rock scurried away. "What the fuck was that?" They watched the strange creature scuttle along until it burrowed itself in the ground.

"We are gonna have to be real careful what we do in this place," Malcolm warned. "We're not in Kansas anymore. Things here are not the same as back home, and God knows which ones will try to eat us."

Emily stopped and turned around. "I think you're right. We'd better not touch anything that even looks the slightest bit odd. Some small and innocent looking thing could be poisonous." She waved as she saw John and Joe coming up to join them. "If we do need to check something out, we should use the barrel of our gun to poke and prod it." She called out to John, "Everything okay?"

"Yeah, we tossed him through, no problem. I just hope Paulie hadn't left the room to take a piss or anything. The way we had to throw him, he probably hit the floor pretty hard on the other side. Wasn't any time to be gentle about it."

"I'm sure that Paulie is taking care of him right now. We didn't have a choice. He wouldn't have made it out of here any other way." She put her hand on his arm.

"Yeah, I know. He was bleeding pretty badly." John unbuttoned his bloodied shirt. "I think I should toss this and put on a clean one. The creatures here might be attracted to the smell of blood." He used the clean part of his shirt and some water to wipe himself off, then pulled a fresh shirt out of his pack and put it on.

Archer looked concerned. "John, you notice the spheres that are following us? What do you think they could be?"

"No idea, but let's keep moving. Maybe they'll get tired of tagging along."

"Where are we headed?" Max was looking toward the hills.

John surveyed the landscape. "I've never seen anything like this before. There aren't any landmarks. If we have to come back here, I honestly don't know how we'll find it again." He looked up at the hazy sky. "There aren't even any stars here."

Taking his compass out of his pocket, he opened the protective cover. "Maybe we can use the compass to help." He turned in a circle to verify that it remained consistent. "I can't guarantee this is what we call North, but at least it's pointing at something that appears to be constant. If we head toward whatever it's pointing at, we should be able to come back to this place by heading South. That'll help… Shit!"

"What's wrong?" Charles was trying to get a look at the compass.

"Uh, it just changed. It's pointing over there now." He indicated the direction with his hand. As they looked, they realized the spheres were nearly on top of them.

"Damn, we are gonna have to deal with these things," John grumbled. "Em, get ready with the sidearm. Max, Joe, grenades. Charles and I will power up the ultraviolets. Arch, you got the sword? Here they come!"

The spheres floated up slowly to surround them. "Don't do anything until I give the signal."

"Signal?" Joe asked. "We didn't mention any signal."

"Just keep your eyes on me, and don't do anything until I do."

As the spheres hovered around them, there were sounds of whispering voices. Quiet at first, they became louder as they moved in closer.

"Are those damn things talking?" Arch didn't want to talk too loud. He stood ready with the sword.

"It sounds like they're saying something, but I can't make it out." Charles had no idea that a sphere was hovering just behind his head. It was close to touching him when he began to feel a tingling sensation on his scalp. It felt like a bug was crawling across his head. He reached up to knock it away.

"Charles, no!" Emily tried to warn him, but it was too late. As his hand brushed up against it, the sphere glowed even more intensely. He jumped away as it began to vibrate.

Everyone watched in awe as the sphere unfurled to form a human. Before them stood a balding and overweight middle-aged man. Completely naked and rather stunned, he seemed thoroughly disoriented. "Oh my God!" he exclaimed, "Is this for real? How did I get here? Who are you people?"

They were all speechless for a moment until Joe spoke out. "Hey man, can you cover your junk or somethin? Geezus!"

The man stared at him like he didn't understand. Joe pointed down at his no longer private privates. "Uh, can you handle that python before it puts somebody's eye out?"

Finally, the bewildered man looked down at himself. Quickly covering the offense with his hands, he muttered, "I'm sorry, I-I didn't know…"

"That you're buck naked? I'm afraid we have more important things to worry about right now." John had questions, so he asked them directly. "Where are we exactly? What is this place?"

The man shrugged his shoulders. "I'm not sure. I haven't been here before, at least, I don't think so."

"We're looking for somebody. A man about this tall…" Emily held her hand about a foot and a half over her head, "with brown hair and greenish brown eyes." She felt silly saying it, but since this guy was naked, she added, "He's probably wearing clothes."

The man looked at her with a vacant stare as she spoke.

"That's a hell of a description!" Max laughed.

"Look, Max, if you think you can do better, then step up. Otherwise give me a minute, all right?" she glared at him as he backed away from her with both hands up in a gesture of surrender.

The man continued to try to cover himself. "I-I don't know for sure. I'm sorry, I haven't…"

"Been here long, right, we got it." John was frustrated.

"Yes, that's right, but how did you know that?" He looked at the group suspiciously. The man was obviously confused and still disoriented.

While the naked man was speaking, the orbs continued to hover just overhead. The team paid closer attention to them now in order to avoid touching another one. They were not aware of the creature flying toward them. It wasn't until it struck the naked man in the back that they realized a new peril was upon them.

The wingless creature resembled a snake, but was shorter and thicker than any snake they had ever seen. It did not have wings, so it was not obvious how it was able to fly. Perhaps it had been launched somehow. Regardless, it had certainly found its target.

The man was struck just below the base of his neck. The creature had hit him hard enough to send him stumbling forward for several feet. It latched onto him with four talon-like claws causing the man to scream in agony and begin to convulse. Desperately clutching at his back, he was unable to free himself of the vile little beast that had attached itself to him.

"What the fuck is this shit?" yelled Max as he jumped back from the man who had now fallen to his knees.

"Please, help me!" he shrieked as he tried to pull at it. He thrashed back and forth until his screaming began to fade as flickered like a fluorescent light bulb about to burn out.

"Somebody do something!" Emily cried out as she stood helplessly witnessing his agony.

Bullets and explosives were out of the question. It would likely kill the man and risk hitting the crew. It dawned on John that he was holding one of the ultraviolet lamps in his hand. He quickly switched it on, but it was too late. The man was pulled into the creature's mouth as easily as a tissue being sucked into a vacuum cleaner hose.

The beast turned toward John with its mouth still open, its rippling throat visible as it clicked its talons menacingly. It quivered a moment before making its move. John held the light steady as the creature flew toward him. He saw a row of small beady eyes encircling the gaping mouth just before it exploded in a cloud of dust.

"Holy hell! Looks like the light works!" Joe congratulated him as he stepped up to examine the dust settling to the ground. "Damn. What the hell do you think that thing was?"

"No idea, but it was ugly as shit." John shook his head.

"Was that guy was a ghost or something? Maybe that snaky bastard is a ghost eater. Some weird shit, for sure." Malcolm offered, not quite joking. He looked around at the other spheres. "I mean, it attacked the dude, but not the spheres. Why? You think these things are souls or something?"

"Well, there's only one way to find out." John reached out to the sphere floating closest to him and touched it.

"No, John. Don't…" Emily was too late to stop him.

John stepped back, signaling the others to stay back as well. The sphere shook. It took on an intense glow and then began to unfurl just as before. When a very gorgeous naked redhead was standing directly in front of John, there was a chorus of comments from the other guys.

"Holy crap!"

"Wow!"

"That's what I'm talking about"

Until Emily shut them down with, "Come on! Like you never saw a naked girl before?"

"Joe hasn't, at least not outside of a strip club anyway." Max cracked and the guys started laughing.

At first, the woman stood blinking. She had the same confused look as the man had earlier, but gradually her face took on an expression of concern. After looking around in all directions, she began to speak. "They can't get to us when we are in the protected state. I have to be careful now."

"Protected state?" John was beginning to feel that something was wrong here aside from all the alien creatures and the weird happenings of this world.

"Yes, the others who are attracted to you as I was. We're safe unless you make contact with us. Please don't touch anyone else. I will ask them to leave." With that, she raised her hands and called to them. The spheres formed a circle around her. She spoke to them in a whisper and they whispered back to her. A few moments later, they slowly floated away across the landscape.

When she turned back to the group, Emily asked, "Where will they go? What did you tell them?"

"When we are floating in that state, we see living humans as a bright light. As we passed into this world, we heard whispers to follow the light to our destination. We were unsure what it meant and followed many lights that led us nowhere. We seem to be hopelessly lost."

She looked around nervously and went on. "It has been many days since we have seen a light anywhere away from the killing grounds. We thought we had found the way out. That is how we came to you." She looked quite sad at that point. "I'm afraid we will never be able to leave this place."

"Can I touch you?" Emily asked, "I mean, are you real, like solid?"

"I… don't know. You can try."

Emily cautiously reached out and touched the woman's shoulder. "She's solid." The woman stood silently as Emily turned to the group. John was staring at the woman, perhaps a little more intently than he was aware, and Emily gave him a look that shot right through him, "Excuse me, Mr. Hazard. See something you like?"

At that, the woman turned to John as though she recognized the name. "Hazard… that name sounds familiar but I can't remember why."

Suddenly and simultaneously, John and Emily recognized the woman. For Emily, it was the memory of a photo she had found in a book in the bookcase at John's apartment the first night they spent together. For John, it was the recollection of a suspect in a murder case. The bodies, the spirits, the box, the baby and then… the name slipped out, "Rachel?"

"Oh great!" Emily huffed. "So *that's* her name then? Of course, you would remember."

"Do I know you?" Rachel asked innocently.

"Uh… not exactly," John answered, blushing at the embarrassing moment from his past to which Emily referred. There would be a lot of questions to answer now. He was sure of it. Emily slipped the strap of her backpack off her shoulder and knelt down, setting it on the ground. She dug through the bag, looking for something.

Joe stepped up to Rachel. "Hey, Red, my name is Joe." He gave her a nod and offered his hand in greeting. He wanted to find out for himself whether she was indeed real or if his hand would pass right through her. And, if she was real, well then… he might just try to get to know her better.

Rachel reached to take Joe's hand. When his hand met hers, he bent to kiss her delicate fingers. Suddenly, the guys seemed much more interested in the mystery woman. She had proved to be very real and they moved to introduce themselves as well.

Meanwhile, John stepped back to have a word with Emily who was pulling some clothes from her pack. When she found what she was looking for, she flung them at him with some force. He caught them and held them up, asking, "You think these will fit?" He made an effort to strike a tone that would not offend and further irritate her.

"You mean, will her huge, perfect tits squeeze into my small little shirt? Probably!" She was obviously upset. "If you can get those guys to back off and quit slobbering all over her, maybe she can try these on."

She tied the flap on her backpack and looked over at the guys falling over each other to get closer to the curvy woman. "Hey guys, how 'bout doing the decent thing here? Stand down and let the girl put on some clothes." Blank stares followed John as he handed Rachel the items.

Forty-Four

Emily had to admit that Rachel looked amazing in the borrowed jeans and Metallica t-shirt. Not only did her ass fill out the slim jeans beautifully, but her breasts were pressed into the shirt revealing her erect nipples. The guys were having a difficult time not being distracted. John needed to do something quickly to get everyone back on track or their mission might fall apart completely.

"Okay, everybody, let's not forget what we need to do." He looked around at the faces of his team, and except for Emily who had him locked in her steely glare, all the guys were still staring appreciatively at Rachel. No matter where they stood in the circle, their heads were turned toward her. He cleared his throat to get their attention. "Stay with me, guys. We need to find Franks location. Find out if he is being held hostage and get him out of here, whatever that involves."

They all nodded as he spoke. "One other thing. Rachel is the closest thing we have to a guide here. Try to remember that. We need her help."

He tried to lower his voice to prevent Rachel from hearing. "Even if she does look good to you, she is a spirit, which means she is dead. Any plans you might have for some romantic interlude on this mission are not going to happen. Save your fantasies for some real women back home, dogs." That got their attention. They knew the mission came first, it always had.

John was well aware that Emily was watching him closely. She followed him as he got up close and looked into

Rachel's gorgeous green eyes. "Do you remember how to get to the place you called the killing grounds?"

"I can't say I remember exactly, but I can feel myself being drawn there. We spend most of our time trying to resist the call, but many have been lost to it. Why would you want to go there?"

"Call?" Emily was trying to understand what was happening here. "Can you actually hear it calling to you then?"

"It is not exactly something we hear. It's something we sense. While we can hear the people who are imprisoned there, we also feel and smell them no matter where we are. Something about them makes us ache with desire. They are living like you, but they don't last long. Their spirits seep out of them. When that happens, we feel drawn to them. Then they are gone." She glanced down at the ground then again at Emily. "It is difficult for us to resist going there, but since it always ends badly, we try very hard to stay away." She looked at Emily with sadness in her eyes, "Am I making any sense?"

Emily nodded. She wanted to know if the team could be susceptible to this call. "How would we know if any of us are experiencing it? What would it feel like?"

"You will not have this experience unless..." She became very somber. Emily assumed that she was about to say, *unless they were dead*, but then she continued, "I have seen others here who have been captured in ambushes. They get caught while they are sleeping, or walking through the forest. Some are brought here from the other side through the machine. They are drained by the things that feed on them. That's when we feel the most irresistible pull."

"So you've seen the portal?" John asked.

"Portal? Is that what you call it? No, I haven't actually seen it. I have heard the prisoners in the pits talk about it.

I've seen the creatures that use it. They go through and bring back the living – men, women and even children. They usually bring back one or two at a time, but occasionally, even more."

"You mean, they're bringing people to this God forsaken place from our side?" Emily was visibly shaken.

John tried to find out as much as possible. "We had to use special computers and a lot of electricity to open the portal. Do you have any idea how do they do it here? Is there electricity? Technology, like computers? I can't imagine…"

"No, those things don't exist here. I believe they use…" She looked as though she might cry. "Us. We are pure energy to them."

"You? They use ghosts to power the portal?" Max asked. "Holy shit! So the thing that came and ate that dude…"

"Many here want to use us. Thousands arrived with me when I came." She looked off in the direction that that spheres had gone. "Many more pass through all the time."

"So, the spheres… other spirits are at risk of being trapped here if they are around us?" Emily felt true concern. "I'm glad you made them go."

"It will be hard for them to stay away. They are so drawn to you. I hope they don't feel compelled to return." Rachel turned back to the group. "They believed you were their light and could take them away from here. Now they're lost again." Sadly, she looked over at John. "What do you want me to do?"

"You said you are drawn to the killing grounds. Can you feel it now?"

"I have felt it since I first arrived."

"We need you to follow your feelings then. We need you to take us there. It's possible that our friend was captured and is being held there. Will you help us?"

"Yes, but please control your expectations. Your friend may already be dead."

"Yes, we realize that. We're here to take him home either way." John looked around the barren landscape and wondered what else they would encounter. "It's what we do."

Forty-Five

Frank sat in the pit reserving his energy and contemplating his next move. He was waiting for the beast that was guarding him to take a break or at least walk away for a minute. He had spent hours hollowing out hand and foot holds as high as he could reach. His fingers ached from the effort and his fingernails were cracked and crammed with dirt. As long as the Cyclops stood guard, there was no way he could climb out to escape.

He wasn't even sure that he *could* escape. And, if he did, where would he go? He had awakened in this pit, brought here from somewhere by something, or was it someone? He had no way to know where he was. He wasn't even sure how long he had been here. His watch had stopped working the moment he had passed through the portal. The only thing he knew for sure was that he was hungry and parched from thirst. It was obvious that he was being held prisoner, but no one had offered him any food or water since he had regained consciousness.

"Hey, you ugly bastard!" Frank tried to get his guard's attention. There was no sound above. Was this the opportunity he'd been waiting for? He went to the side of the pit and tried the first foothold of his makeshift steps. It crumbled a bit under his weight, but seemed to stabilize. His heart was pounding. Carefully, up three steps he climbed using the handholds. One more step, and he was just able to peek out over the edge.

The guards were nowhere to be seen. Could it really be? He put his hands out over the top and pulled himself up and out of the hole. Squatting low, he checked in both directions for some way out of this place. He needed to get back to the portal. The question was *which way to go*? All around him were dozens, if not hundreds of holes just like the one he crawled out of, but who or what was in them? Staying low, Frank duck walked, half crawling to the next pit and peered over the edge.

Huddled against the wall was a boy, his arm wrapped protectively around a girl. They were not moving at all. Frank wasn't sure they were even alive. Their emaciated faces reminded him of cancer patients in their last hours of suffering. Reduced to skin and bones, their eyes were sunken and ringed with dark circles.

Leaning over the pit, he whispered, "Hey, can you hear me?" Without a sound, the boy opened his eyes and looked straight into Frank's. "I can help you get out of there. Do you know how the guards get in and out of these holes? Do they have some kind of ladder?"

The girl's eyes opened. She stared wistfully up at him. The boy moved his mouth to speak, but no sound came from his parched, cracked lips. Frank tried to assure them, "Look, I'm gonna try to find a rope or something to get you out of there."

He stood up and scanned the area in front of him. It appeared he was at the edge of a compound. There was a makeshift fence. The way it was made, it looked as though it was there to keep something out, rather than keep prisoners in. Every five feet or so, there was a sharpened pole that jutted outward at an angle toward the field beyond.

Frank was putting two and two together. *If that fence is there to keep someone or something out, and the beasts inside here are as big as giants, then what in God's name could be out there?* He shuddered at the thought of it.

Turning around, he checked to see what was behind him. For as far as he could see, there were pits scattered across the field and no sign of a ladder or a rope. The sheer magnitude of this place struck him like a punch in the gut. Whatever or whoever was in all of these holes would probably die there from thirst or starvation if nothing else. There was no sign of food or water anywhere.

Off to his right, in the distance, he could make out a large structure, *or was it more like a hive?* As scores of creatures, a multitude of sizes and kinds of them, flowed from the holes at the sides of the structure, he began to remember. He had been there before. Like a nightmare, the details were fuzzy. Before he could piece it together, the creatures fanned out across the landscape. *Were they coming for him? Had he set off some kind of silent alarm?*

Frank decided not to hang around and find out. He ran for the fence, dodging between the pits that were before him. He glanced into each hole as he ran past and his blood ran cold each time he saw another person. Every pit held someone. Smaller children were in groups of two or more. It broke his heart, as he realized he would have to abandon the two children who had been in the pit next to his. He hoped he would be able to return somehow and make good on his promise to help them.

Some prisoners seemed relatively healthy and watched him as he passed, but most were emaciated and near death. He wasn't sure if he had seen it clearly, but it appeared there was something attached to the backs of some. It wasn't a backpack, that was clear, but more like some kind of large slug-like creature. No way in hell was he going to stop running long enough to find out what it was.

Undoubtedly, the fence was much taller than it had appeared from a distance. As he approached it, he realized that it must have been built by the Cyclops. They would have scaled it according to their own size. He judged each of the lower cross beams to be a little better than a foot apart from the next one up. It had been quite some time since he was in boot camp, but he remembered the drills.

When he reached the fence, he put his arms out and vaulted between two beams. He landed on the other side and discovered there was a slope surrounding the compound. It was steep enough that when he hit the ground, he twisted his knee. Pain shot up his thigh as he got to his feet and tried to run. *Oh shit!* He grabbed his knee and felt around trying to figure out whether he had any severe damage or it was merely a strain. If he was lucky, he would not be incapacitated.

He pushed himself up and tried to put weight on his injured leg. It wasn't good, but he thought he might be able to loosen it up if he walked on it for a while. In the distance, he saw a stand trees, at least they resembled trees, and so he headed in that direction though he wasn't quite sure where he was going. With every step, a jolt of pain shot through his knee. He worked hard to push it from his mind and kept moving forward toward the trees. If he was able to find help, he swore to himself, he would return to rescue the others who were being held captive.

Forty-Six

Rachel led the search party into the strange forest. They had come upon it quickly, *or had it come upon them?* John wasn't quite sure. He thought the trees had been farther in the distance, but it must have been an illusion. Nothing in this place was as it seemed, and he was growing more apprehensive by the minute.

Cautiously, they walked through the scraggly leafless trees. Each one had a combination of weapons at the ready. Some held a rifle and grenades. Others chose handguns and ultraviolet lamps. Archer had a pistol in one hand and his sword in the other.

"If you have to use the lamps, remember not to shine them on Rachel," John warned over his shoulder. "We don't know what effect it might have on her, and we can't afford to lose the only one who knows anything about this place."

"Are these trees familiar to you, Rachel?" Emily was walking with her now. "Are we headed in the right direction?"

"I remember passing through trees like this. I think the killing grounds are just on the other side of this forest." She put her hand to her head as though trying to focus. Checking all around, she said, "Something's coming this way."

"Take cover!" John brought his semi-auto rifle up at the ready. "Which way?" he asked, trying to see what it could be. "Where is it coming from?"

"I can't tell." She closed her eyes and clutched her head. "It burns... It feels so hot inside of my head!"

Max whispered and pointed at something coming through the trees. "I see it, boss!"

It was difficult in the strange twilight to tell exactly what was headed their way until it was nearly upon them, and then, there it was! Coming fast upon them was a Cyclops, just as Archer had described in the strange story about the cavern in Iraq. It was much bigger and even more terrifying than it had sounded back in the lab. Emily had to force herself to keep from screaming as they scattered for cover behind the gnarled trees.

Moments passed. She exhaled slowly, thinking they must have gone unnoticed, until the thing let out a roar and slammed headfirst into the tree where Max was hiding. It hit hard, nearly felling the tree, but Max remained silent and still on the opposite side of the trunk. Convinced the beast was after him, he wanted to remain undetected for as long as possible.

Suddenly, strange creatures began to drop from the branches of the tree from above. They were half the size of a man, with a narrow torso and two arms with long claws curved into a hand-like configuration. The creatures had no neck, but a head of sorts, flattened where a face would be. Where one would expect to see legs, there was a thick coil, maybe a tail that moved it along like a snake.

One of these alien beings fell within a few feet of where John was standing, and he jumped back. He wasn't sure what to expect. He could see the sharp claws at the end of each arm as it scrambled to balance itself on the ground. Obviously, the creature was not built for walking, and it didn't appear to be situated to fly, so what was it doing in the tree? Its eyes were like dark black beads protruding from its misshapen head, and it stared at him for a moment before its tail coiled beneath it. All at once, it lunged out toward John, springing as though on a pogo stick.

"Oh shit!" He backpedaled as fast as he could while the ugly bastard slashed at him with its claws. It stopped its offensive long enough to strategize a new plan. Its small round mouth opened and closed while scores of tiny tentacles whipped in and out. John was nearly hypnotized by the strange sight and inadvertently let down his guard. When the beast finally made its next leap, he barely composed himself in time to duck out of the way. He moved just in time to send the creature crashing into the tree behind him.

Meanwhile, the Cyclops was reaching around the trunk of the tree with its long arms. It nearly got hold of Max several times. Dodging and staying just out of reach, he managed to avoid being caught. The Cyclops slammed itself against the tree again causing more of the creatures to drop. One of them landed on Malcolm. He screamed for help as the beast dug its claws into his shoulders and wrapped its tail around his waist just below his ribcage. As the tail tightened, it squeezed against his diaphragm and crushed the breath from his lungs. He let out a rattling gasp as he struggled to break free.

More of the snake like creatures were dropping from the trees and hopping at them from all directions. They used their coiled tails like personal trampolines to jump several feet in the air. No one could get to Malcolm without being assaulted. Chaos was all around them as the Cyclops roared with rage. Max had slipped out of his reach yet again.

Archer kept a watchful eye on the Cyclops even as he fought off an ugly little jumper of his own. At last, he felt he could free himself to help. Raising his sword above his head, he charged the giant. He jumped in the air with a rebel yell and brought the sword down with tremendous force, thrusting it between the Cyclops' shoulders. It was as though lightning had struck it from within. The wound in its back emitted a burst of light and the Cyclops exploded.

Archer raised his sword victoriously as the dust swirled around him and settled to the ground.

Max stepped from behind the tree, a look of shock and gratitude on his face. Without uttering a word, he pointed at Malcolm who was flailing his arms, trying in vain to throw the creature from the tree off his back.

"Get this fuckin' thing off…" His voice was cut off mid-sentence as the beast put its mouth against the back of his neck.

John and Emily fired their handguns, but the bullets went right through the jumping monsters that had them surrounded. "What the hell is it with the fuckin' aliens in this God forsaken place? They won't fuckin die!"

Archer had been impressed by the effect that the sword had on the Cyclops and figured it could be more useful than guns in this situation. While the others continued firing their weapons, he powered through the chaos, swinging the sword from side to side until many of the creatures lay in pieces squirming on the ground.

Archer's success gave the team time to rethink their options for fighting off the creatures. "Try the lights." One by one, the team holstered their guns and searched their packs for the ultraviolet lamps. Charles had been holding one the whole time and powered it on, turning it toward the crazed jumpers. The light had little effect until the creatures were as close as eight feet away. At that point, one that he had targeted began to swell like a balloon, quickly stretching its rough gray skin. In a matter of seconds, it burst into dust.

Now he was confident he could help Malcolm. "I'm coming to help you, Mal. Hang in there," he shouted, seeing that the creature that had attacked his friend was solidly attached to his back. With a crazed look in his eyes, Malcolm slowly moved to take his handgun from its holster.

Emily was standing nearby, directing her immediate attention toward exterminating the monsters that were trying to corner her. She was using her UV lamp to drive them back and eliminate them. Malcolm turned and raised his weapon, aiming directly at the back of her head.

"No!" Charles yelled, "Mal, what are you doing?"

When Joe saw what was happening, he stepped up behind him and took hold of his arm. He quickly pulled it upward. Again and again, the gun discharged into the trees above them causing the shattered branches to rain down on them. Joe wrenched the gun from Malcolm's hand and threw it aside.

Emily hadn't realized what was happening behind her until Joe yelled, "Emily, use your lamp on this son of a bitch!"

She spun around to see Joe holding Malcolm with his back toward her. The creature was clinging to him, sucking the life from him. *To hell with this!* She stepped forward and held the lamp inches from the creature. Almost immediately, it burst into dust and Malcolm's legs buckled under him as he fell to his knees.

There was still work to do, and Joe saw that Emily was attending to Malcolm. He turned back to the fight at hand. The lamps had been quite effective against the snake-tailed beasts. Their numbers had been greatly reduced. Joe and the others continued using the ultraviolets until the last of the aliens bounced away in a mad dash for their lives. The team was left to stare at one another in disbelief.

"What the hell were those things?" Charles brushed the dust from his clothes.

"Somebody give me a hand." Emily called to them. She was kneeling next to Malcolm, trying to hold him up. She wanted to inspect him for injuries, but was having little success.

"I have no idea." John said, answering Charles' question while he moved to assist Emily.

When he got to Malcolm, he pulled down the collar of his shirt and exposed his neck. "Look at this." On the back of Malcolm's neck were ten small puncture wounds arrayed in a two-inch circular pattern. "That damn thing was trying to feed on him!"

Rachel had hidden herself in a tight clump of trees during the fray and had remained there unnoticed. As she moved to stand behind John, she commented, "Trying to feed?" She had to warn them.

"Glad to see you're still with us," John greeted her. His relief was sincere. They needed her.

"I could not afford to be seen by any of the creatures you encountered here," she said. "That clutch had your friend under its control. Clutches like that attach themselves to humans and feed on them. I've seen them do it at the killing field. When they have had their fill, they excrete some type of fluid that is used by the one-eyed creatures. They drink it."

"Kind of like ants and aphids?" Emily had learned about that on a nature show she liked to watch. "They eat the sap from plants and then ants farm them like cattle and feed on the fluid they produce."

"I'm not sure if it is exactly like that but I've seen the big ones pull a clutch off a human and drink from the tip of its tail. It is disgusting I can assure you. They usually sleep awhile after that."

Malcolm was still shaking off the effect of the clutch. "It was strange. Like I could hear that thing talking to me, and then I couldn't control myself any more." He offered Emily an apology. "I'm sorry, Em. For some reason, it kept telling me to shoot you."

"I never saw that part of it or I would have kicked your ass myself. Don't feel bad about it though. I believe it wasn't your fault. All that matters now is that you have your head on straight so we can get on with this." She felt kind of sorry for him. He looked shaken up.

"I'm okay now. I'm glad to know you understand, but I really felt like I *wanted* to do it. I wanted to please that clutch thing more than anything else." His eyes got a little misty. "I never felt anything like it before. It was horrible, but at the same time, it was wonderful. It was… I felt like I was… I don't know how to say it…"

"We need to know, man," John encouraged, putting his hand on Malcolm's shoulder.

"It was like I was stoned, ecstatic really." He looked a little sheepish as he glanced around at the group. "Like an endless orgasm, I didn't want it to stop. I couldn't control my own body."

"Heroin is like that," Joe volunteered.

"The worst thing about it was that I was completely under its spell. I couldn't control anything about what was happening, or…" He dropped his head in shame. "Maybe I could, but I just didn't want to. I'm not even sure now."

Emily glared at him as though she wished he'd stop talking now. She couldn't believe he would kill her just because some fucking thing on his back was juicing him and telling him to do it. At the same time, she knew how men were about sex. Some of the most devastating wars and heinous crimes throughout history were byproducts of men's sexual desires.

"I am sorry, Emily, really."

He sounded sincere enough, but after he had told the story from his point of view, she made her mind up not to let her guard down around him. Who could know for sure if the effect had fully worn off? "We'll just need to be more careful around those things if we run into them again. Have the lamps ready," was all she said.

Rachel seemed nervous. John knew enough to pay attention to the slightest change in her demeanor. "Someone is coming," she said. Her voice was calm and matter of fact. It sent a chill down John's spine.

"Someone or something?" Emily was looking all around.

"Someone like us… I should say, like you. It's human."

"Are you sure?" John pulled his binoculars from a pouch on his belt and scanned the woods ahead. She was right. There was someone coming. He watched as the person wove through the trees. It appeared to be a man, and he seemed to be injured.

John wiped the sweat from his brow, and lifted the binoculars again. "Holy shit! I think it's Frank!" He stuffed the glasses back in their pouch and started walking toward Frank. No one hesitated to follow.

Forty-Seven

Frank looked like hell, but he was alive, and John was more than relieved to see his friend. Although he hadn't been missing long, he had aged noticeably since the last time John had seen him. It was good to know that he and the rest of the rescue team hadn't gone through the portal and lost one of their friends to a critical injury, only to find out it was already too late.

John wasn't satisfied to simply say hello. He greeted his friend with a big bear hug. In fact, it was hugs all around. As soon as everyone had an opportunity to welcome Frank, he asked for water. He drained half the canteen before he was ready to answer any of their questions.

John was the first to ask, "Where the hell were you, Frank?" That opened the floodgate. The questions were flying fast, and Frank looked from person to person as they fired them off.

"I was held in some kind of compound… they had me in a hole in the ground."

Rachel interrupted, "The killing grounds."

"Yeah, that's exactly right, a fitting name for it. There are creatures there, Cyclops like the one we encountered in the chamber in Iraq. There are creatures that I've never seen before. And, I gotta tell you, I wasn't the only prisoner. They are holding a lot of people."

"What do you mean people? People like us?" Emily was worried. "How did they get there?"

"I'm not sure what was going on. Most of the time, I was held in some kind of pit. I can't remember how I got there. I have a vague recollection that I was taken to some kind of processing building first. Maybe ten or so other people. It was dark. Something in the ceiling and along the walls was glowing. Everything is hazy in my mind now. Might have been some kind of animal. They moved."

"What happened to your leg, brother?" Max referred to Frank's obvious limp.

"I twisted my knee when I jumped the fence. I think it'll be okay. It doesn't hurt as much as it did when it first happened, so it can't be too bad."

"You'll feel that shit in the morning." Joe nodded, rubbing his elbow. He knew what he was talking about. "Although, how do we know when it's morning is here? Day, night, it all seems the same to me in this shithole."

"You got a point. I don't even know how many days it's been since I got here. There's no sunrise, no sunset. There's only a hazy glow all the time." Frank looked up at the reddened sky.

"Days? You think you've been here for days?" John shook his head. "I don't think it's even been twenty-four hours yet."

"Hell, it seems a lot longer than that. I wondered why it was taking you guys so long to come for me." Frank looked worn out. "I thought that damned machine had blown up and my ass was gonna time out back in that hole. I decided to attempt an escape rather than let them feed on me."

Charles lifted his head now. He had been rifling through his pack. "Feed? You mean those…"

"Yeah, there are creatures that feed on you. They certainly control you. The fucker that jumped on my back had me walking right into the camp, but I gotta tell you, the sensation I had at the time…"

Emily cut him off, "Yeah, yeah, we know. Mal had one on his back, and he tried to kill me just because it told him so."

"How'd you pull it off him without killing him? The one on me wrapped itself around my chest. When I tried to resist, it damn near squeezed the breath out of me."

"Ultraviolet portables," Joe said holding up his handheld lamp. "Good thing you had enough for all of us. This shit does a number on those jumper dudes."

"We call them clutches because of the way they hang on you," Rachel informed Frank. "The others feed off what comes out of them."

"Who is feeding off what?" Frank noticed Rachel now for the first time. "And who are you?"

"That's Rachel," John replied. "She's dead, so don't get excited. She's some kind of spirit or ghost from what we know. She was bringing us to the compound to look for you."

"Well, thank you for offering to help." He held out his hand to shake hers and was surprised to find that she felt very solid for a spirit. "My name is Frank. Nice to meet you."

"Yeah, so John knows her from when he was a cop," Emily offered.

"Detective," John corrected.

Frank heard the tension in Emily's voice and looked over at John. "Nice coincidence, huh?"

John took hold of Emily's hand. "She said you were probably in that place. I guess she was right on the money."

"Yes, her instincts were correct, if spirits have instincts, that is." He smiled at the stunning redhead trying to figure out why he had a strange feeling about her.

"Look, Frank, we came from that direction." John was pointing back over his shoulder. "I think we need to get back to the portal and get our asses out of here."

"I think you are assuming that the portal will be in the same place as when you came through, but it moves. I don't know if we'll be able to find it again." Frank's brow furrowed with concern.

"Yeah, we figured out that it moves. There seems to be quite a time difference between this world and ours as well." Charles was pacing and keeping an eye out beyond the trees. "When we came here, we stepped through only seconds apart, but by the time each pair came through, minutes had already elapsed and the portal had moved."

"And we may have lost Clark." Archer interjected. "Some fucking creature came up from beneath the ground and…"

"It was some ugly monster fucker, came out of the ground and buried its tentacles in his arm. We ended up having to cut it off to free him." Joe gestured as though holding a sword. He made a slicing motion.

Archer finished the story, "We had to run a long way to get to the portal and toss him back through. Figured Paulie could probably get him to a hospital in time."

"Well, we might not have to find our particular portal." Frank was checking the area around them as he spoke. "Remember I said there was a… I guess you could call it a building, but it's more like a giant anthill. I'm sure I saw a machine there that was similar to the one I built."

"What, they have computers here?" Emily kept looking up into the branches of the trees expecting something to drop on them at any moment. The last thing she wanted was to be taken by surprise by something dropping on them again.

"No, not computers. There was an opening in the wall and one of the Cyclops came through with a little boy. From what I could tell, they are going into our world and bringing people here. I'm sorry. It's like trying to remember a dream."

"Are they rounding us up like cattle or something?" Max offered with a nervous chuckle.

"I didn't see them eating any humans. It was more like…" Frank hesitated, unsure of how to put it. "It's more like they're extracting something. When that bastard attached itself to you, Mal, didn't you feel something being drained from you?"

"Yeah, I guess so. After they got it off me, I felt real tired. I figured that the high was wearing off."

"I'm not sure if it's hormones or adrenaline or what. Whatever it is, I guess they need it. And, they need us to get it." Instinctively, Emily reached for the back of her neck as Frank continued, "Thing is, they only put those clutches on your back for a while. After that, they take them away somewhere. I guess they extract whatever it is, like milking a cow, and store it somehow."

"That's some sick shit!" Joe spat on the ground. "So that kid they had, they…?"

"Probably. That's why we can't just go back and look for our portal. Aside from the fact that we don't know where it is, we can't just leave here knowing what we know. We have to help these people."

"Mother fu…" Joe started.

"Frank's right," Emily interrupted. She circled the team, searching the faces of the group. "It could happen to any of us, a member of one of our families, our neighbors. I say we kick some monster ass and save some people."

"Look, baby, we've been in the shit before, and we had to make some tough decisions. You know how much I regret that we had to leave some folks behind up in those woods. But, this time, I'm with you." He looked around at the rest of the team. "We've got to step up and save as many as we can. Let's kill these monster fuckers and save some people. If we don't, they're just going to keep coming for us." John held his hand out into the middle of the group like a quarterback in a huddle at the biggest game of the year. "Who's with us?"

Without hesitation, Emily and Frank stacked their hands on top of John's. In an instant, the others stepped up and added theirs to the stack. A thunderous "Oorah!" echoed through the forest.

John walked over to a low hanging branch and snapped it off. "These are some strange ass trees. This branch is almost like glass." With that, he hunkered down and started drawing out a plan in the dirt.

Forty-Eight

Between what Frank had seen and what Rachel could verify, they estimated that the killing grounds stretched across an area of fifty to a hundred yards or more. It had a hive-like structure that was built both above and below ground. It seemed to be the living quarters for the Cyclops and other creatures. The field surrounding it consisted of containment pits dug at least ten feet deep and spaced evenly. Viewed from above, the field would have probably looked a little like a honeycomb.

Each pit held from one to five people. Frank's theory was that small children were held in groups while adults and teens were kept alone. They might be found in pairs, but only if they were weakened or injured. Healthy adults would be capable of working together to climb out and escape their fate, so it seemed they were destined to die alone.

John drew up his plan based on the intel related to the changing of the guards. It seemed to occur at regular intervals. Frank had noticed the pattern during his time as a captive. The field had been abandoned by the guards during the time it had taken him to escape.

John scratched a diagram in the hard ground showing positions and movements. He used some round stones to represent each person and moved them about to show how the operation would be timed. Everyone was a bit startled when the stone representing Archer sprouted legs and scuttled away. "Uh, that is not part of the plan, Arch," John chuckled before continuing.

"We'll split into two groups. Each group will wait at opposite ends of the compound until the guard change begins. As soon as the field is clear, we'll start sweeping toward the center and meet here in front of the hive." He pointed at the circle he'd drawn to represent the building.

"As we advance, we'll gather as many people as we can rescue from the pits. All able bodied survivors will be armed with any weapons we have and together we will storm the hive. We'll kill every fucking monster that tries to stop us." He looked around at the faces of the crew and saw nothing but nods.

"Once we get inside, we need to locate the portal as quickly as possible. We open it and get everybody the hell out of here. We have no way of knowing if these assholes have a way to call for reinforcements. I don't think we want to hang around to find out."

Frank interrupted, "When you came through, how long were you able to keep the portal open? In my first try, it crashed after about five minutes and I had to let it cool down."

"I'm not sure. We didn't go back after we threw Clark back through. We can't even be sure he made it."

"Oh, that's great. That's what I love about this paranormal shit, nothing is ever as it seems and you never know what's gonna happen next." Emily seemed anxious, but she surprised the guys when she added, "So fuck it, nobody lives forever, right? I guess we'll do whatever it takes."

John smiled at her, "That's the attitude we need to get back home." He continued to map out the plan. "We'll plant a few charges of C-4 in the hive and on the portal. When the last person goes through, we'll blast the shit out of that place. Those bastards will never come and play in our backyard again." Everyone agreed it was a good plan.

Frank wanted to make one thing clear before they were in the heat of the battle. "We can't use any explosives while we're in the open area until we're sure that the holding pits are empty. We don't want to kill innocents if we can help it."

"If we get the people out of the holes first, we can push the guards in. We could take out quite a few of those bastards that way." Joe's suggestion didn't yet resonate, so he elaborated. "If we can pull some of the stronger folks out, we can give 'em some rope or something so they can help the others. That would get more out of the holes. Then, if there's any of those bastards around, we can push them in and use our grenades to blow their asses up."

"Grenades just slow them down, remember?" Emily reminded him about the Cyclops in Iraq. "Monsters like that, and the one that got Clark, they were blown apart and then somehow came back together. The only permanent solutions we've seen so far are the UV lamps and the sword."

"Okay then, how about we blow the shit out of 'em? Then we light 'em up to keep 'em from coming back. Easier to deal with little bits of 'em anyway."

John smiled, "I don't give a shit what anyone says about you, Joe. Sometimes you are pure genius." He put his hand on Joe's shoulder and gave him a friendly slap on the back. "So, that's what we'll do. We'll push 'em in and blow 'em up, then we'll use the lights and keep right on kicking ass and taking names."

The group was so involved in their planning session that they had let their guard down. Rachel stood slightly outside of the group and had been keeping a watchful eye, but even she had been distracted by listening to the plan. She never noticed the creature flying toward them through the woods.

It hit her hard between her shoulders, its talons digging deep into her neck and knocking her to the ground. Everyone turned to watch in horror while the creature thrashed back and forth on her as she lay screaming.

"Oh no!" yelled Emily, scrambling toward her and feeling around in her backpack to find her UV lamp. Rachel's eyes bugged out as she vainly tried to pull the creature off.

John fell to his knees beside her and tried pulling it, grabbing it in the middle of its swelling body. It squirmed in his hands as Rachel's body started to flicker. He pulled harder, but the creature was locked on. It seemed to be fused to her neck. Rachel's body began to stretch and distort. Before anyone could help, she was sucked into it and was gone.

Rachel's clothes crumpled to the ground, as Emily switched on the lamp and turned it toward the monster before it could make its getaway. "Die you motherfucker!" Emily shrieked. She held the beam steady and moved in closer. When it fell to the ground, she held the lamp directly against its body until it exploded into dust.

She dropped to her knees, sobbing. Holding the shirt she had loaned to Rachel, she hugged it to herself. "She didn't deserve that! Nobody deserves to go out like that!" She looked over at John with tears streaming down her cheeks. "I don't want to die here, John. What the hell is this place?" This was the straw that had broken her spine of steel.

John knelt down beside her and put his arms around her. "Shhh, Em." He rocked her in his arms. "It's gonna be all right, baby. As soon as we rescue as many people as we can, we're going to get the fuck out of this insanity."

"You really think we'll get out of here, John? Be honest. We don't even know where *here* is! What if the machine Frank told us about doesn't work?" She looked into his eyes. "Promise me, John. Don't let me die like that. Promise that you'll help me."

"Of course, Em, I will protect you with everything I am…"

"That's not what I'm saying! Promise that if we can't get back, you won't let me suffer."

The impact of her request finally hit him, and his eyes welled up as he understood her meaning. She would rather he take her life quickly if things went south on them. He gave her a squeeze and replied, "Don't you worry. We're getting' out of here if I have to blow a hole in the fucking universe!"

"I know you will, baby. I trust you." She rested her head on his shoulder and closed her eyes for a moment.

Joe nudged Archer and whispered, "Remember what I told ya? Chicks aren't cut out for the frontline. When the going gets tough they…"

Emily opened her eyes and glared at them. "Fuck you, Joe." She stood up with new resolve. Brushing herself off, she proclaimed, "Let's go kill these bastards!"

Forty-Nine

Frank led them back toward the pits where he had been held. He was limping but seemed to have recovered much of his strength. As they reached the fence that surrounded the area, they divided into two groups. Each team headed around the perimeter to opposite ends of the killing grounds. Since John's team had the furthest distance to cover, they decided to use the flare gun that Malcolm was carrying to signal the other team when they were in position.

As they skirted the tall fence, the holes in the ground that Frank had described came into view. It was impossible to determine how deep they went. There were no guards in sight except a few bulbous creatures pushing themselves along with short fleshy legs. It was uncertain what kind of role they played. Frank hadn't mentioned them.

It appeared that the unfamiliar creatures were headed to what Frank had referred to as the "hive." It was an accurate description. The large hill-like structure was made from mud and stone. They could see the main entrance and various other openings. From their vantage point, it was difficult to gauge how large the openings were or what could be lurking inside.

John hoped they would not meet with resistance while they climbed through the fence. As he checked to see what they could be facing, he was immediately overwhelmed at what he saw. Frank had only described what he had been able to see from where he was held captive. There was a second field of pits that stretched before them for another hundred yards or more.

"There is no way we can cover this whole area while fighting off these bastards and still get us all out of here!" He wiped the sweat from his forehead using the back of his sleeve. "We'll clear what we can, and then we're out of this shithole!"

Emily stayed close to him. After what had happened to Rachel, she seemed somewhat subdued. John knew she was preparing herself for the fight, and whenever the shit started going down, he could count on her to be fighting right next to him.

***

Frank's team had been waiting at the other end of the field for nearly half an hour. He and the guys were on their stomachs trying to remain hidden from view. Joe broke the silence to lament, "Shit, we forgot the prayer!"

Frank thought back on all the successes his team had experienced when they followed their pre-battle rituals. This was no time to be changing things up. "You want to say something quick, Joe?" He understood how important it was to keep his men focused, so he nodded to the others and bowed his head.

Joe started, "Lord, we don't know where we are today, but you do, and if this is hell, well, we know we better survive and live to change our ways. Nobody wants to end up in a place like this for eternity. Anyway, wherever we are, we got a job to do. Please help us save as many of the folks being held here as we can, and kill any of these bastards who get in our way, cause we know that you …" the others joined in as he finished, "send no angel to do the Devil's work."

Just then, a flare popped into the sky at the other end of the fence. They ended the prayer with a hearty *Oorah!* and jumped to their feet.

***

At the other end of the field, John and Emily climbed over the lower beam of the fence with Malcolm, Archer, and Charles close behind them. Just a few steps into the field, they were able to get a look at the first row of pits. John and Emily stared down into the one nearest their entry point. An emaciated man lay at the bottom, still and lifeless. Emily lowered a length of rope over the side. His dark, vacant eyes looked up at them as John called, "Hey buddy, we're here to help you. Here, grab the rope."

It was plain to see that the man wanted to move toward the rope that was dangling within arms reach. However, he could only manage to lie helpless and try to will it to come to him. He didn't have the strength to stand or even lift his arm to reach for his best chance of escape. He tried to speak, but no words came out. His lips were dry and cracked, and he looked as though he was crying, but no sound came from his gaping mouth.

"You're going to have to help me, okay? I can't jump down there. If you stand on your knees and tie yourself to the…" John was horrified as the man convulsed and died.

In shock, Emily stood motionless holding on to the rope. John was signaling her to move to the next cell. "Em, come on. This is only the beginning. We're going to have to stay strong." His voice was low as he moved to the next pit.

Worse than the last hole in the ground, the next one held children, two boys and a girl. They looked to be about eight to ten years old. John's heart sank as he realized the little girl had a clutch on her back. He went around the side to help Emily with the rope as she called softly to the children, "Grab this rope, sweeties. We're gonna get you out of here."

The boys just stared at them as they tossed the rope as close to them as possible. The oldest boy reached for it and attempted to climb up. John took up the slack and began pulling him out. His feet were about a yard from the bottom when the little girl let out a shriek and ran toward him. Possessed with extraordinary strength for one so small and sickly, she pulled at the boy's legs. She dug her feet into the dirt wall in an effort to hold him down.

"Kick her," John yelled at him. He was pulling the rope up and nearly had him to the edge to pull him out. The girl was obviously under the control of the clutch. She was hanging on to one of his legs. Thrashing around like a fish in a net, she occasionally reached out to claw at the boy. It hindered John from pulling the boy out and over the edge.

Emily unclipped the UV lamp hanging from her pack. "Screw this!" She yelled as she flipped it on and aimed it toward the clutch on the girl's back. Its tail had been wrapped around the girl's waist. It began to unwind, twitching violently before exploding into a cloud of dust. The force of the blast was enough to knock the girl back into the pit. Stunned, she hit the ground hard.

Now the boy could easily scramble up and over the side. At the edge of the hole, he remained on his hands and knees breathing heavily. The struggle had taken a toll on him, and he was obviously exhausted. Emily tried to help him stand while John threw the rope to the second boy.

"Come on kid, let's go," he called, but the boy just sat on the ground next to the girl, staring at him.

The older boy tried to speak, but his throat was too dry. Emily offered him some water from her canteen. After two gulps, she pulled it back. "Not too much at first," she cautioned.

His mouth moistened, he was finally able to tell her, "He won't come out without her. She's his sister."

Archer, Malcolm and Charles had pulled several men and women from the ground. Some of them were strong enough to help pull others out. Still others helped to care for the weaker ones, pulling them up to help them stand so they could advance with the group.

***

At the other end of the field, Frank's crew was working their way toward the center. They hadn't been able to pull up many survivors. Most of the prisoners were emaciated or near death, and there seemed to be no way to get them out of the ground or carry them out without losing some of their own.

There was another reason they chose not to pull out some of the prisoners, and they were all pretty freaked out about it. Not all of the captives were human. Some appeared to be alien. Not small, thin, grey aliens. These had fur and the face of a large cat, such as panther, yet stood upright like a man. Their claws were quite long though attached to very large hands instead of paws. The men had never seen or heard of anything like it before.

Philip had already discovered that the cat creatures were not friendly. He had tried to help one of them climb out, but quickly withdrew his hand and dropped the rope to avoid the long claws slashing at him. Apparently, it did not trust his intention and seemed determined to fight him off. When he told the rest of the team about his experience, no one attempted to help any of the others.

Between the nearly dead humans and the aliens, one or two out of every five prisoners were being left behind. Even if they could rescue the aliens, how could they hope to communicate with them or help them return to *their* world? Worse, they could end up defending themselves against them and weaken their defenses before the real battle began. Still, it troubled Frank. The aliens were as much victims as the humans. Yet, he had to keep the success of the mission foremost in mind.

Some minutes later, Joe offered a suggestion. "What if we pull someone up who has the clutch thing attached to them, then frag it in front of one of the cat dudes. Maybe if we do that, they'll understand why we're here."

"You think they are intelligent enough to understand that?" Max was lowering a rope into a pit to pull out a woman.

"Hell, I figured it out, didn't I?" grinned Joe.

"You got a point there!" Philip teased, helping the woman step away from the pit. "I got a guy right here with one of those things on his back. He doesn't appear to have much fight left in him. We can use him to try your theory." He was already tying a knot in the rope and leaving a large loop at one end. Twirling it like a cowboy's lariat, he swung it around three or four more times before letting it fly. It landed around the man and Phillip pulled it tight.

"Give me a hand, Joe." He was holding the rope taut to keep it from slipping loose.

Joe stepped up and grabbed hold. "Let's go!" he shouted, and they began pulling the man up from the hole.

The man was bent over and twisting uncomfortably in an effort to free himself. The pull on the rope against his weight kept him secured, even against the will of the clutch on his back. When they got him to the surface, they got their first close-up look at a clutch. They could see how it was fastened to the victim.

"That's some disgusting shit!" Joe groaned, as he looked closer at the man's neck.

"I'm surprised it isn't trying to escape," Max called over to him. He had backed away and could only observe from a distance. "It must not be aware of what we're planning. Come on, drag it over here, and try not to let it get loose."

"No worries, it ain't getting loose." Joe pulled the rope and dragged the man to the edge of one of the pits that held a cat-man.

"Hey, ugly!" Joe yelled down at it. "Check this out!" When he was sure the creature was watching, Joe unclipped the lamp from his belt and held it out behind the clutch.

Suddenly, the parasite began to respond and tightened its tail around the man's chest. Joe could hear the whoosh of air that was being squeezed from his lungs. It dug its sharp claws deep into his shoulders and blood started to flow. When Joe switched the lamp on he counted, "One, two, three," and the sucker exploded.

After the obliteration of the clutch, the creature in the hole tilted its head and went wide-eyed, as though curious to know how the man had done it. Joe eased the victim to the ground, making sure he was okay, before turning back to the beast in the pit. He held out the light in his hand, "Works like a charm!" he yelled, and flashed a big grin.

A few beats later, the creature smiled back disclosing row after row of teeth. It mimicked Joe as it vocalized, "Ike a tarm." It held is arms out toward Joe, putting its clawed hands together as though grasping for the rope. It was trying to make a climbing motion.

"Son of a bitch," Joe said, scratching his head. "This dude wants me to help him out!" The man beside him was sitting up and regaining his senses after being freed of the clutch. "Hey Phil, what say you and me oblige him?"

Fifty

A crowd was beginning to form behind John's team as they pulled more and more people from the holes. All were suffering from varying degrees of starvation and dehydration. Though they had some supplies of food and water, they refrained from sharing it right away in the event that their departure from this place was delayed. They knew too well that anything could go wrong.

For now, however, their rescue plan was being executed to the letter and without interference. John was beginning to wonder if Lady Luck had decided to smile on them after all. That is, until the sirens began to wail from somewhere within the hive. It started out at a low pitch and volume, and then it cranked up.

"Doesn't that sound like an air raid siren from one of those old war movies?" he asked.

Malcolm agreed. "Yeah, I used to watch a lot of those old black and white flicks when I was a kid. It sounds just like that."

Emily moved up next to John. "That can't be a good thing." John didn't respond. He was looking out in the distance ahead of them as creatures large and small came pouring out of the hive. Some on foot, some flying. They were about to find out what they were up against.

"Step it up! We need to get as many as we can out of those holes before they get here!" John looked out over the group that had already been rescued to see who could help. "Anyone who feels they can help us move the people to safer ground needs to step up and do it, NOW! Gather up the ropes and have them ready."

About a dozen men and women took the ropes from his team and moved to help the weaker ones move back. One man who had emerged to lead them nodded toward John to indicate his cooperation.

John continued to bark out the orders, "I want all of the kids and the weaker adults twenty yards at the rear. The rest of us will fall back about ten yards so we get some space between the remaining captives and our frontline. If we go to grenades, we're gonna need room to toss 'em without killing the ones who are still in the holes. As a last resort, if we can't hold these fuckers back… everyone, please, run for your lives."

***

At the other end of the field, Frank and his men had pulled out several of the alien cat-creatures when the siren sounded. Frank shifted into high gear. "Joe, if you can communicate with the cat-men you've been rescuing, now would be a good time to explain that we need some help."

"I got this, boss," Joe said, tapping one of the creatures on the shoulder. He proceeded to pantomime to the alien how to pull others out of the pits using the rope. The creature watched him for a minute, and then shook its head. It pointed at the weapons as if it understood what they were.

"You want to use some heavy artillery?" Joe pointed at the guns. He yelled at Frank, "Hey, Frank, the furry dude wants to use the automatic weapons. Whatcha think?"

"We don't have time to train 'em on those. Bad idea."

While Joe's attention was directed at Frank, the alien snatched the AK47 right out of his hands and looked it over. It pulled back the slide to cock it.

"Holy shit! The bastard knows his weapons." Joe nodded his approval as he smiled at his new friend.

"I hope he's friendly," Frank cautioned

No sooner had the words left Frank's lips, than the first wave of the attack was nearly upon them. In the lead was a team of creatures flying toward them on leathery wings tipped with deadly claws. Screeching loudly as they began their assault, they made a direct dive at them from above. Weapons were tossed to two more cat-men. Handguns and ammo clips were caught in clawed hands and the three aliens, armed and ready, formed a firing line beside the other men.

As they opened fire at the aerial threat, Frank helped pull more people and aliens from the ground. "We gotta fall back for the next wave. We'll need about fifteen to twenty yards between us and the pits ahead of us. Let's go!" The newly liberated captives were retreating and looking over their shoulders as they watched the attack coming from behind them.

As they dropped back, the team at the front was blasting the winged creatures from the sky. When the bullets pierced their small bodies, they burst like water balloons, fell to the ground and lay twitching as though they were dying. Whether dead or not, they appeared to be out of the game.

"Do you know how to use grenades?" Frank yelled at several newly rescued volunteers. "Pull the pin, let the handle drop, count to three, and throw." He held one in his hand and demonstrated. "Watch our backs, and don't let anything get close. Otherwise, don't do anything with the grenades until I tell you. We need to have a clear area so we don't blow up any innocents. Save them for the ground attack."

The men nodded and accepted the bag of grenades, distributing them among themselves. Though weakened by captivity, they were happy to fight. Now they would have an opportunity to exact some kind of revenge on the monsters who had held them prisoner here.

***

Meanwhile, John readied his team for the wave of flying creatures coming at them. He could hear the gunfire from Frank's crew but had no idea how they were doing. *Shit, I hope those guys are firing over our heads.* He looked around to be sure that no one had been hurt before focusing again on preparing for attack.

"I think we should try the lamps, John. There are too many to shoot them all out of the sky. We could end up using most of our ammo on these things." Emily was shouting over the noise of the shrieking creatures.

John nodded. "Damn, girl! Why didn't I think of that?" Turning to the team, he barked, "Lamps up everybody, and wait for my signal. If you don't have a weapon, get back, way back!"

As a hundred or more creatures closed in on the frontline, John yelled, "NOW!" All of the lamps were switched on, forming a wall of purplish light.

The winged beasts were approaching fast and flying higher as they neared. From there, they would dive down like hawks to reach their prey. For a split second, John wondered if their plan had any chance of success. Then, at a distance of about ten feet, the first line of attackers exploded into dust. It was as if they had slammed into some invisible force field, and they were powerless to penetrate.

The dust from exploding creatures was flying everywhere making it difficult to breathe or see what was happening, but the team held fast. The large group behind them stood gaping, in awe of the effect that the lamps had on the creatures. By the time the aerial attack had ended, John's team was bent over coughing up dust. It was covering all of them as if they had just been hit by a sandstorm.

"Shake it off! We gotta gear up for the next round." This time it would not be enough to use the lamps. They would need to use all weapons at their disposal to stop the large creatures now headed their way. He called for those who did not have weapons to move back even more. Some required assistance to do so.

"Anyone have experience with guns?" Archer shouted into the crowd. "Don't raise your hands, just step up." When a handful of haggard looking men stepped forward, he told them what to do. "My team is taking the frontline. Your job will be to keep their weapons loaded. Get behind them and help them reload. Keep the extra ammo in the bags in case we have to fall back. Everyone is depending on you."

Emily and the two volunteers assigned to be her re-loaders were quickly setting up. They laid out an array of guns, ammo clips, and grenades from the small arsenal that she and the others had been carrying. On down the line, the same scenario was playing itself out, each trio wordlessly preparing their arsenal.

"What the hell are they waiting for?" John walked down the line until he was standing next to Emily. "You'd think there's a general up there giving them orders? Shit!"

The sirens sounded again. They could see the beasts beginning to move slowly. As though receiving an order to charge, they sprang into action and began running toward them. They gained ground quickly, running on all fours like dogs, dodging and leaping the pits as they came.

Occasionally, one would fall into a pit. John shuddered at the thought of what would happen to anyone who was trapped there.

He winked at Emily, saying, "Now I'll bet you're sorry you got hooked up with someone like me."

"Well, if I wasn't here with you, I'd probably be sitting in some drab little coffee shop wishing that something interesting would happen." She smiled then as she checked her weapons. "If this is the end, then we go out with a bang. But let me just say, John Hazard, if we make it out of here, this is the last time I'm going to follow you into some alternate dimension to protect your ass. I love you, but a girl's got to figure out just how far she's willing to go for her man."

"I love you too, Em. Believe me, I totally understand."

They could feel the ground shake as the beasts closed in. John turned and yelled to the others, "We're gonna do this in a line just like before. If anyone falls, somebody damn sure better step up and take their place. Even if you have to fight with your bare hands, losing is not an option." Everyone, including the volunteers, the injured, and even the children nodded their agreement.

"Your most effective weapon is the handheld lamps, after that the grenades. You need to be careful with the grenades. After you pull the pin and drop the handle, get it out of your hands in three seconds. Whatever you do, don't let them hit the ground within twenty feet of yourself or anyone else. Try not to throw them past the first three rows of the pits either. Got it?"

Just then, he saw the gang of Cyclops that were coming behind the dog-like beasts. They were slower, but a horrible sight in their own right. John had the terrible realization that many, if not all of his crew and the people they had rescued, were likely to die.

Fifty-One

The charging beasts would reach Frank and his team in a matter of seconds. Although smaller, these things reminded him of the two-headed dog that had attacked him in the chamber in Iraq. They were running fast and leaping over the pits as they came. Frank could see the Cyclops coming behind them. The one-eyed beasts had to run with more care to avoid falling into the pits.

The three cat-faced aliens at the frontline had managed to pluck two more of their own from the pits after the barrage of flying death had passed. However, the amount of weapons Frank could make available to the newly rescued was minimal. The cat creatures were skilled marksmen, but they also wasted bullets on creatures after they had already hit the ground. Frank needed to keep a handle on the weapons and inventory of ammo in order to save what they could for the raid on the hive.

"Does anyone have grenades to spare or some bayonets in case we have to go hand to hand?" Frank asked his men.

"We should have brought swords like the one from the chamber. There were four of 'em in the armory. I was gonna grab one but decided not to add the extra weight to my pack. Arch has the only one we brought," Phillip told him.

Frank took him by the shoulders and looked him in the eyes. "The one that Archer brought, is it the *real* one or a replica?"

Phillip shrugged. "I don't know. They all looked real to me."

"No matter, I guess. We don't have it, and right now, there's no way to get to it. We gotta focus on surviving this." Suddenly, there was gunfire. The cat-men were already in the thick of it.

"Drop back! We need more room!" Frank yelled at the people behind him.

No one hesitated to move except the cat-men. Apparently, they didn't understand the order and remained in position. He was trying to tell them that their bullets would not stop the larger creatures, but the thunder of gunfire drowned out his useless attempt at communication.

"Damn, they need to move back," groaned Joe as he took action to warn his new friends. Rushing forward, he tapped one of the creatures on the shoulder and tried his best to tell him. He motioned him to move back, but still he didn't move.

This was no time for subtlety. Joe wrapped his arms around the alien and threw it over his shoulder. As it howled in surprise, he quickly retreated to where the rest of the group was waiting. Now the other cat-men followed. They took their places with the men who were holding grenades, pins pulled.

***

John's team could see the four-legged beasts coming close and braced themselves as the battle was about to begin. Automatic weapons discharged, and the slugs were penetrating the monster's flesh. It merely slowed them down, but none fell. They just kept coming. The frontline seemed to be mesmerized. Finally, John yelled, "Throw the fuckin' grenades!"

Almost immediately, the grenades rained down on the charging beasts. The fastest of the creatures were moving too rapidly. They had already passed through the grenades before they blew. However, beyond them, a large section of attackers suddenly vanished in a shower of gore that flew in all directions. The frontline dripped with bloody splatter.

"Use the lamps NOW!" John shouted over the noise.

The crew switched on the UV lamps as they dodged the beasts that had run through the grenades. Most of them exploded in a cloud of dust, but there were too many to deal with at once. The snapping, snarling monsters were now in their midst. Several rescued prisoners fell as the creatures slammed into them. Like wolves, they made quick work of their victims, ripping open their abdomens and tearing them limb for limb. Bloodcurdling screams of horror came from the horrified bystanders as limbless torsos were tossed aside like broken dolls.

As the others moved through the carnage with their lamps, Emily found one of their own, his eviscerated torso hanging halfway into a pit. "Oh God! John! They got Malcolm!" She bent over him to see if there was any chance he could still be alive, but as she leaned forward, she could see his intestines trailing down the pit walls into a pile at the bottom. Lightheaded, she shifted her feet to maintain her balance. She knew that she had to keep her wits. Things were happening too fast now to be distracted by grief.

As she turned back, she saw his lamp lying on the ground nearby. They would need as many ultraviolets as were available in this battle. As she reached to get to it, something hit her from behind and sent her tumbling. Her own lamp fell from her hand as she rolled across the gore splattered ground. Feeling the beast behind her, there was no time to retrieve it. She slid to a stop and rolled to her back to face the reddish sky.

As her attacker moved into view, it opened its massive jaws, preparing to rip her to shreds. Trembling with fear and anger, she kicked and fought against its rubbery flesh. Closing her eyes to meet her fate, she pummeled it with everything she had. Suddenly, it exploded in a cloud of dust above her. As the dust settled to the ground, she glimpsed John's smiling face and his hand reaching out to help her. "You okay, wild thing?"

As she got to her feet, she made a half-hearted attempt to wipe the dust and gore from her face and arms. "Enough of this bullshit. Where's my light?"

John smiled and nodded at her, pointing to the lamp. He picked up Malcolm's light as she went for hers. John called to a man who was backing away from one of the creatures. He tossed him the lamp. In a single fluid motion, the guy caught it, switched it on and shoved it into the open maw of the beast as it charged him. Seconds later, the dust cleared and the man had moved on to help some others.

With the assault still in progress, the ground began to squirm beneath their feet. The bits and scraps of creatures dispatched by grenades were reforming with mind numbing speed. Those who were wielding the lamps had their hands full obliterating the new, even more terrifying beasts as quickly as they sprung up, while continuing to battle with the ones that were ripping a path through the survivors.

John silently prayed his thanks to God that Emily was okay and was back to sweeping the area with her lamp. He could see her stopping to help others who had been injured during the fight.

In the chaos of the battle, Archer had dropped his lamp and pulled his sword as the battle came too close. The blade was effective as he hacked and stabbed, leaving dismembered monsters in his wake. He was glad to have the sword for what was coming next, a pissed off wave of eight foot tall, four-armed Cyclops.

***

Meanwhile, Frank's team had effectively used their grenade defense against the initial ground attack. Wriggling bits of creatures were strewn everywhere and the rescued were helping to clean up the mess with the UV lamps that Frank had obtained from John.

"I don't know how we're going to stop those things," Frank nodded toward the Cyclops making their way toward them. "We're almost out of grenades, and I'm not sure how much longer the lamps will last. We need to make our way to the hive. We can't keep this up forever."

"There's still a lot of people in those pits," Joe pointed out toward the ones they had yet to check. "A lot of 'em might be kids."

"I get it, Joe, I do, but if this keeps up much longer, we won't be able to hold 'em back. We'll all end up in a hole, one way or another."

"We need the damn cavalry right about now," Joe said, "or maybe some kind of miracle."

The odds were not in their favor and Frank agreed that Joe was right. They did need a miracle, but in this crazy place, it wasn't something any of them could expect. He knew the worst was yet to come, but he wasn't the type to give up.

"Fuck this mess! Let's kill these bastards and go home!"

Fifty-Two

Emily was terrified as the wave of Cyclops closed in. She tried to hide her fear from John, but he knew that look and the desperation in her eyes. He remembered well their last adventure when the aliens had attacked them in the clearing just before Frank had shown up to rescue them.

"Hey." He nodded over at her. "We're going to make it out of this, Em. I can feel it." He smiled even as he braced for the assault.

"Use the grenades!" He gave the order, perhaps a moment too late. Like a tsunami, a wall of Cyclops plowed into them swinging and grabbing at them with a four-armed fury. The sheer size of them struck fear into the embattled team's hearts, and it drove them back.

A group of volunteers behind them were tossing grenades and trying to use their lamps. The grenades worked to blow the monsters to pieces, but the Cyclops were much larger than the four-legged animals that had come before them. It took longer for the lamps to have an effect. The delay gave the giants all the time they needed to knock the lamps aside. The embattled humans were about to be exterminated.

From the corner of her eye, Emily could see John fighting. From what she could tell, he was doing all right. She was dealing with one of the giants herself, dodging its grasp as she held steady the beam of light. As she moved away from its reach, she caught sight of John again.

"John! Behind you!" she screamed as she saw a second beast coming up behind him. He was distracted by the one

in front of him, and the warning came too late. It snatched
him up like a rag doll and shook him above its head.

Archer saw what was happening and tried to fight his
way over to help John, but he was also surrounded by
swinging arms and gnashing fangs. Bracing himself in a
wide battle stance, he grabbed the sword with both hands.
He prayed loudly as the sweat dripped from his brow,
"God, if you're there, I could use some help right about
now."

Tightening his grip, he prepared to fight to the death.
One of his fingers slid over the red stone embedded in the
hilt at the base of the blade. Immediately, a beam of white
light shot from the blade. It was as bright as a hundred suns
and spread out from the tip of the sword in a swath about
two feet wide. *PHHHHTT! PHHHHTT!* As the
approaching Cyclops crossed the path of the light and
exploded into a brilliant cloud of dust, the one coming up
alongside it exploded as well.

"Oh shit!" He held the sword out, amazed at the beam
of light coming from it. Until now, no one had realized the
potential of the weapon he held in his hands. It just might
be enough to put an end to this battle. As he heard again
the sound of his friend screams, he snapped back to face the
horror of John's predicament.

***

At the other end of the field, grenades were flying and
gore was raining down on Frank's men and the rescued
group that battled with them. Large chunks of exploded
Cyclops flesh were in the process of reconstituting into
something much larger and more deadly. The ground
churned with slippery ooze. Everyone involved in the fight
was slowed by the slippery footing. Trying to use the lamps

to clean up the mess was a daunting task made worse by the oppression of the enemy that continued to come at them.

As bad as things were for them, a greater threat was looming not far away. The piles of tissue that had fallen into the pits were boiling with activity. Frank first became aware of what was happening when a massive tail rolled out from a pit about twenty feet in front of him, landing with a loud thump on top of the upper torso of one of the dismembered Cyclops.

Two women had been working feverishly to drag the lower half of the Cyclops away before it could fuse together again when the tail slammed down and sent them diving for cover. It looked like the tail of a gigantic snake as it lifted again, absorbing the Cyclops into its flesh.

Frank's mouth opened as the beast continued to rise from the ground. Backpedaling quickly, he realized that this was no snake. "My God!" he screamed out as the dragon emerged from the pit. Gore and debris took to the air, flying toward the dragon, melding into it, and increasing its massive proportions.

***

All eyes turned toward John. He had been a respected and admired leader here in this world. Their blood ran cold when they saw the Cyclops biting down on his abdomen. It was shaking its head as though trying to rip out his guts.

"Drop him, you motherfucker!" Emily screamed as she ran toward it trying to zap it with the light from her lamp. It was no small relief when she saw that its sharp canine teeth were imbedded in John's ammo belt.

John was not about to cooperate as he was being torn apart. He felt for his knife and unsheathed it. As the monster opened its mouth to bite down on him again, he rammed the blade into the large single eye, popping it like a balloon. Howling in pain, it nearly dropped him as it shook its head, clapping two of its hands over the ruined eye. Now John was dangling by one leg and he believed he could break free, but his attacker would not let go. It desperately grabbed at him and caught hold of his shirt, raising him to its gaping jaws to bite down on his thigh.

Archer was making short work of the giants surrounding him. Any creature native to this world that was touched by the beam of light emanating from his blade was instantly obliterated. Now that he could manage it, he turned the blade in John's direction, but it was too late. Blood was running from the beast's mouth as his friend collapsed.

The sword was humming as the shaft of light made contact with the creature that had been attempting to kill John only a fraction of a second earlier. It exploded as John dropped six feet to the ground and lay motionless like a broken toy as the dust floated down around him.

Emily rushed to his side and began checking him for injuries. She found some serious puncture wounds on his leg, and he did not respond when she tried to move him. "John! We need to get going. I can't carry you, John!"

Hoping to rouse him, she slapped his face gently, then again harder, but it was no use. She felt his neck for a pulse, and though it was weak, it seemed to be steady. He was bleeding badly from his leg, so she reached into the bag lying on the ground next to him, searching for something she could use as a bandage. When she saw that the bag contained nothing but ammo, she fought back tears as she tried to think of something to use to stop the bleeding.

"God help me," she cried out in anguish as she watched the life of the only man she had ever loved bleeding out into the dust of this alien world. It was in that moment of total surrender that the answer came to her.

***

Archer was a killing machine, clearing the field of every creature that could claim this world as their home. He had discovered that if he constantly held his thumb on the stone, he began to feel as though he was being drained. Therefore, he had begun to use short bursts instead.

After rescuing several people from experiencing the same fate as John, he stepped to the front of the group and mowed down the horde that continued to rush at them. Creature after creature was pulverized as the battle continued. The beasts seemed to have reinforcements coming from the other end of the field as they became aware that their comrades were getting their asses kicked.

The beam from the sword was beginning to fade as Archer became exhausted. "I need help!" He was having trouble holding it up. "This thing is draining me," he gasped. It seemed to him that the weapon's supernatural power was drawn from the person wielding it, and he was just about out of gas.

Emily looked up as she heard Archer calling for help. She had taken off her shirt and torn strips from the lower half to bandage John's leg. She had managed to stop the bleeding, but he lay very still. Pulling what was left of her shirt back over her head, she found there was enough of it left to cover her breasts. With nothing left to do for John, she looked around for someone to stay with him while she tried to help Archer. Not far away, Charles was using his lamp to destroy leftover pieces of the creatures that continued to try to combine to form new ones.

"Charles, I need you NOW!" she shouted. He quickly handed his lamp to a nearby woman and hurried to help Emily.

"John has been hurt. Please watch over him for me." She was on the move before he had even reached her. "Archer's fading out and I gotta help him finish this."

Fifty-Three

The Cyclops kept on coming, but Archer's efforts had reduced their ranks considerably. When Emily reached him, he was on his knees and the intensity of the light coming from the sword had diminished greatly. He could barely hold the blade above his waist.

"What's happened to you?" she asked as he looked up at her with sunken eyes.

"I think the sword's power is coming from me, like I'm some kind of battery. Here, take it. Finish the job, or pass it on to somebody else, 'cause I'm about used up." He let go of the stone and the beam immediately stopped. He turned it around and held it out to her, grip first, until she took it from him.

"I don't know if I can do this." She turned the blade over in her hand to check it out. "How does it work?"

"Just… Hold it…" he gasped for breath now, "with both hands. Press your thumb into that red stone. Use your whole hand if you need… it's like the damndest flashlight you've ever held." As he finished the sentence, he slumped down on his heels.

She was amazed at how much he had seemed to age during the battle and wondered what it would do to her if she did what he said. He looked… *really* old. How quickly had he aged? Could it take her life? She came to her senses as she realized that the group was being overrun again. She was not willing to let them all die here without trying.

Holding the sword tightly with her right hand, she wrapped the fingers of her left hand around the hilt and squeezed down on the stone. Immediately, the beam shot out of it hitting Archer right in the chest. She let out a squeal and released the stone. "I'm sorry!"

"Please don't stop." he smiled, "That feels really good!"

She hit him with the beam again for about three seconds and he rose to his feet. The color had returned to his face as he laughed, "Damn, that's incredible, I feel like a kid! Are you good?"

She was stunned at what had just happened. Checking herself, she nodded, acknowledging that she felt fine.

Archer stepped up to her and put his hands on her shoulders. He turned her in the direction of the oncoming attack and gave her a reassuring rub. "Switch that thing on, girl. It's your turn to play exterminator."

He admired Emily's grit. She squeezed the stone and activated the sword, looking fierce as she shot it out across the field destroying one after another of the hideous monsters.

"I'm going to help John," Archer assured her. "Don't worry. We'll get him out of here." He patted her shoulder as he turned to leave. "I know you can do this. I've heard the stories about you. You're very special indeed."

He started to walk away, but he called back to her, "…and Emily, if John ever breaks your heart, I'm going to be first in line to help you get over him."

She tilted her head in John's direction, motioning him to keep moving. "Yeah, right. Go on now. I've got this!" She was determined to get the job done as she spun on her heels and moved forward into the fray.

***

Frank's crew was out of grenades. It had taken all they had to wipe out the first wave of runners and most of the Cyclops. As the dragon rose from the pit, they tried shooting it, hoping at the very least to slow its growth, but it continued absorbing the gore of other creatures into itself. It was growing rapidly, and Frank realized there were only moments left to stop it somehow. Otherwise, they would surely be killed.

"What the hell do we do now, Frank?" Joe was starting to move the group of survivors back and away from the danger. "Man, I was afraid this thing was gonna be a dragon, and it's the biggest damned dragon I ever saw!"

"You were thinking about a dragon?" Frank called back.

"I saw one in a movie once, just like that one. It was so cool, I even got a tattoo." He pulled up the sleeve of his shirt, revealing a dragon tattoo that bore a striking resemblance to the monster that was about to destroy them.

Had the creature read Joe's mind as it formed from the gore left behind by the others? In this alien land, anything was possible. When he considered the incident in the chamber back in Iraq, maybe the monster knew he had a fear of dogs and formed itself into that two-headed dog. Maybe these shifters could assume a form taken straight from the mind of their enemy, extracting fear in whatever form was present and duplicating it.

"I guess it's too late for you to think about kittens," Frank yelled as he backed away from the dragon. It stood about thirty-five feet above ground. There had to be at least eight to ten feet more below ground level, and it was pulling itself out of the hole. Except for the fact that all the bits from the field were still flying toward it, the thing was nearly complete.

"Everybody, RUN!" Frank ordered as he turned to retreat. That was when he heard the sweet sound of a woman's voice.

"It's time for you to die, you fucking pile of reconstituted shit!" It was Emily yelling at the dragon from behind. The monster turned its giant head to see what was making the noise, but it was not distracted enough to give up on Frank and the others. She might have been nothing more than a cricket chirping at its feet.

Emily activated the sword and held it above her head. She fired it straight up into the sky like a warning shot. As bright as a spotlight at a used car lot, it illuminated the entire area. Frank and the others turned to see what was happening. Though the dragon had chosen to ignore her before, the light caught its attention now, and it spun around to face her. It pulled its head back, roaring and lunging at her.

Emily showed no fear as she charged forward. Like a warrior goddess, she shouted as she brought the beam of the sword down, slicing the behemoth in half. The blade left an explosion of dust in its wake. She continued to slice through each quaking inch of its body until nothing remained above ground. Then she stepped up to the pit and vaporized every bit of what was left.

By the time she was finished, a storm of dust was swirling and falling to the ground like snow. It settled over the people in Frank's group until everyone was coughing and choking as they brushed themselves off. When she was certain that no enemy creature was left standing, she removed her hand from the red stone and lowered the sword to rest.

Fifty-Four

The exhausted team and ragtag group of rescued prisoners literally jumped for joy as Emily lifted her arms to the sky and let out a victory yell. Quickly, they gathered up their weapons and packs, ready to beat a path to the building known as the hive. Emily hugged them all as they gathered around her. Finally, Frank joined her at the center of the crowd.

He raised his arm to get their attention before he began. "First of all, I want to thank you all, and I mean everyone. And, Emily, you were truly a sight to behold!" He was forced to pause while everyone cheered again. Frank lifted his arm once more, and the field became quiet. "Now, I just want to go home, how about you?" The crowd erupted again.

"Here's what we're going to do. Emily, Joe, Archer, everyone, we're going to advance to the hive. We need to do some recon and find out as much as we can about this place before we go in. The rest of you, please, we need to help as many prisoners left in these God awful pits as we can. Let's get 'em out of there and get 'em back home with us." The crowd cheered again.

Frank spoke quietly with Charles before gathering with the recon team and heading to the hive. It was a long walk across the field before they stood at the entrance. They wanted to be sure that no other threats would catch them off guard before they tried to breach it.

Archer lifted John and carried him forward with the rest of the crowd. Still unconscious and barely breathing, he was being cared for by the same people who had been watching over him on the field. When the rest of the survivors went into the hive, he would make sure John would be one of the first to go through the portal, if there was one.

The remainder of the group followed Max, Philip, and Charles. They were pulling prisoners up from the pits. Those who were hosts to a clutch received a quick release with the pass of a UV lamp over their unwanted parasite. The more people were rescued, the more hands were available to help rescue others. In less than an hour, more than one hundred and fifty survivors were gathered with them in front of the entrance to the hive.

"Is that all of them?" Frank looked to Max for the answer.

"Yes, except there were a lot of them who were either already dead or too weak to move. We had to set up a triage in order to save as many as we could. I hate to leave anyone, but we'd need a med team to save any more." He called over his shoulder at Emily, "How's John doing?"

"We don't really know. His heartbeat is erratic, and his breathing is shallow, but thank God he's still alive!" Tears trickled down her cheeks. No one had seemed to notice that she had been crying. She had hidden it well. "We need to get to that portal as soon as possible. What's the plan, Frank?"

"We're blowing this door and going in." His voice was matter-of-fact as two of the men readied explosive charges and uncoiled a wire to where the detonator was waiting.

"What if it collapses the building? This thing looks like it's made of mud." Emily was desperate to get help for John.

"Hey, why don't we try the lights on it?" Joe stepped forward, switching on his UV lamp and turning it toward the door. "Anybody who's got a lamp, get up here with it!"

Three men stepped forward and joined with Joe to shine their lights on the door. In a few moments, it began to ripple as though made of rubber, but it remained firmly in place.

Without a word, Emily brought up the sword. She activated the beam and aimed it at the door until it began to crack. With a loud boom, it crumbled and fell to the ground. No one could figure out how the physics of this place worked, but they were all smiles now that they could move ahead.

"Joe, when your dad used to tell you that you were good for nothin', he didn't know what the hell he was talking about!" Frank slapped him on the back.

Emily started to move ahead, but Frank held out his arm to stop her. "Not so fast. No wonder John calls you 'wild thing'. This place could be loaded with booby traps. John would not appreciate me putting you in harm's way, sword or no sword."

The tunnel that lay before them was about twelve feet high and just as wide. It curved off to the left several yards in front of them. "I need two volunteers to scout ahead." Frank looked out at the remaining team and waited.

"I'll go. Give me one of the lamps." Archer stepped forward, and took a UV from one of the men standing nearby.

His courage inspired another man to step forward as well. "You can count me in, too, if someone can spare one of those handguns."

"Here take mine." Emily unholstered her weapon and handed it to the man. "I have the sword, I think I'll be okay." She held it up and smiled at him.

Archer stopped to look at Emily as he walked to the front of the group. "You feelin' alright, Em?" He read her face, looking for any signs of exhaustion or battle trauma.

"I'm fine, Arch. Just get us out of here. John needs help." She glanced back to where he was lying. Archer watched her expression change from sadness to determination.

"Okay, everybody," Frank addressed the group. "We're going in. There's no way to know what we'll be up against in there. I need five more to lead us in, and five more with weapons bringing up the rear, just in case they have some kind of reinforcements. Joe, get two strong men to carry John. I want him in the middle of the group. John gets out of here no matter what it takes to make that happen. You people got that?" Everyone nodded and some shouted an enthusiastic, "Yes!"

Joe moved back into the group as requested. He could see the hope in the faces of the people as he passed. When he reached the center of the crowd, he was surprised to find the cat-men there. They were standing off to the side and watching everything that was going on with great interest. They tilted their heads occasionally when the conversations between the survivors would get a little raucous.

"Hey, Cats, give a hand here!" he shouted over at them and waved his arm for them to join the rest of the group. They stood there looking at him at first. With a little more coaxing, they walked over to where he stood. The five of them appeared ready to help, but the language barriers were such that he wasn't about to assume they understood. Still, he was pleased. His alien friends were showing an interest in being part of his team. For him, being a leader to anyone was a new experience, and he was thinking he just might get used to it.

At the entrance of the hive, the group was ready to move out. Two men were struggling to lift John and carry him into position to move with the rest of the survivors. While Joe was trying to explain to his new recruits that he wanted the two with weapons to walk on either side of the group and watch for trouble, they seemed distracted. No matter how loud he spoke, he couldn't keep their attention. They were communicating to each other with grunts and growls that no human could understand.

Joe was about to give up when one of them tapped him on the shoulder and pointed in John's direction. When he had Joe's attention, he looked at his friends and made some sound the others seemed to recognize. Before Joe had a chance to make fun of the way they talked, two of them had moved to where John was lying. They gently nudged the other men out of the way and easily lifted him up from the ground.

Joe was impressed. They seemed to be aware of what was needed, and handled John with care. He was about to tell Emily about it so she wouldn't worry when he was cut short by Frank's shouted command, "Let's move out!"

Fifty-Five

Slowly the group of survivors and their rescuers filed through the wide doorway and into the primitive building. The shuffling of their feet kicked up a light dust that added to the haze as people disappeared into apparent darkness. Inside the structure, there was a dim light emanating from the leaves of tiny plants that dotted a vine growing along the walls. It cast a glow over the group as they moved along. There was an eerie silence, except for occasional whispering, and the muffled sound of their footsteps.

The walls appeared to be carved from solid rock, and though there was no evidence of any blasting or drilling, a swirled pattern lined the walls. It was hard to determine whether machines had been used in its construction or if it had been hand carved. Either way, the creepy environment was all too familiar to the survivors. They had all passed this way on their way to the pits where they most certainly would have died.

In the lead, Archer and his volunteer partner walked cautiously through the tunnel that had turned suddenly downward at about a ten-degree grade. Ahead of them, it leveled off, and they could see the path widening. Suddenly, before them was an entrance to a very large chamber at the tunnel's end.

Frank, Emily, and the others had been following at least ten feet behind the duo leading them. They could see the chamber ahead, but it was difficult to tell whether it was free of any threat. The dim light didn't give them much contrast to identify objects, and though it looked clear enough from where they stood, Emily had a sudden twinge in her gut.

Archer and his partner stood at the entrance, hugging the walls on either side as they surveyed the room. There seemed to be no sign of a threat. The area before them was free of any obstruction that could hide an ambush. Archer signaled back to Frank and waited for his response. Frank considered for a moment and moved closer to see for himself before he made his decision. Watching for any movement, he finally decided to proceed and nodded his consent to his scouts.

Archer and the man slowly entered the chamber, walking a few steps into the center of the room. They stood surveying the floor for anything that might be hidden underground. The creature that had attacked Clark was fresh in his memory and Archer knew that this place could hold any number of hidden threats. The floor looked solid enough.

"Let's stay close to the walls at first, then we'll sweep back and forth to be sure it's clear before we let the others come in. You got that?" Archer looked at the man for agreement and was dismayed to see the unmistakable expression of fear. He had seen it before in battle and knew that the only thing he could do was to remind the man to be cautious and reassure him that they would get out of here in one piece.

"Hey, buddy, what's your name?" He realized he didn't even know the guys name and here the man was laying everything on the line for the others.

"Mike." The man managed to breathe after responding. "You're Archer, right?"

Archer knew they needed to get moving, but he could see the man relaxing a bit, so he decided to ask him, "Where you from?" He figured he would just start walking when the guy answered and keep the chit-chat going as they finished clearing the room.

"Cleveland. Well, just outside."

Archer turned and started to walk, "Yeah? I knew a guy from Cleveland in Iraq, crazy bastard…" As he took another step, something dropped from the ceiling, totally engulfing him. Suddenly, Mike heard a muffled scream as blood gushed from beneath the umbrella shaped thing that had closed over Archer just above his knees. In a flash, Archer shot toward the ceiling, pulled by some kind of tether.

Mike screamed as the man who had been trying to reassure him now hung above him, legs kicking, in the throes of death. For a second, he froze where he stood. It was a fatal hesitation as another creature fell from the ceiling of the chamber. The sharp lower edge of its umbrella-like body hit him in the shoulder as it fell on him, shearing off his arm. He had been holding tightly to his weapon, and when his severed arm fell to the floor, it reflexively squeezed the trigger. Aimless shots ricocheted off the far wall and sent his jerking arm skittering across the floor, as the umbrella tightened over him and retracted back to the ceiling.

From where Frank and Emily stood, they could see that something had taken their friend and the brave volunteer up to the ceiling to die. Emily tried to process what she had just witnessed. She listened in horror as the men struggled to break free, their muffled screams echoing through the tunnel and blood raining down from above. "Archer!" She managed only to cry out his name.

"What the fuck?" Frank ran to the chamber entranceway holding his pistol in one hand and a lamp in the other. As he leaned in and stole a look at the ceiling, a large clot of blood fell at his feet, splashing up onto his legs. He had not expected to lose one of his best friends here so close to going home. His anger took hold of him, and rather than using caution as he had been trained, he acted on his emotions. He was more than pissed off. He ran through the doorway, raising his gun, crazed and ready to kill anything that moved.

Emily called out to him, "Frank!"

In the dim light, Frank couldn't be sure whether the creature on the ceiling was one giant mass or many smaller individuals. He was certain of one thing only. Right now, his friend was dying and he had to do something. He saw a movement near the ceiling, and before he had a chance to react, a leg fell from above, narrowly missing him as it landed on the floor with a thud.

Immediately, he began firing on the rippling mounds of flesh that moved across the ceiling. The bullets from his sidearm had little or no effect on the massive creature. He dodged to the left and right as several leathery umbrellas dropped around him.

Emily watched from the entryway as Frank fired and dodged the attacks coming from the ceiling. Fear wound its way up her spine and she was growing impatient. She looked back toward the strange cat creatures that were holding John who was strung lifelessly between them. She could feel her heart pounding as she yelled, "Fuck this!"

Breaking free of the group, she ran into the chamber. She passed Frank so quickly that there was no chance of stopping her. Holding the sword above her head, she pressed her palm against the stone on the hilt and the powerful beam shot from the tip of the blade. One of the umbrellas fell toward her before exploding in a blast of dust as she wielded her column of blazing light. She panned the beam back and forth across the ceiling vaporizing everything in its path.

From the relative safety of the tunnel, the rest of the group could hear Emily's shouts. "You fuckin' think you can kill my friends and I'm gonna stand here and not wipe the floor with your ass? You don't know who you're fucking with you piece of shit!" She was swearing at the creature as she worked to eliminate every trace of it. The buzz from the beam of the sword created an unearthly edge to her voice as she worked the entire room, blasting the final bits of it to hell. Clouds of dust settled all around her in the eerie light.

The survivors knew by way the plumes of dust filled the tunnel all the way back that she had killed something much larger than they had seen before. As the haze parted, a dust-covered, crazed looking woman emerged and yelled to the group, holding the blade high, "Clear!"

Frank found what was left of his friend lying in the middle of the floor where he had fallen, broken and disfigured. Not far from him were the remains of the volunteer. There was nothing he could do for either of them now. His immediate task was to lead the rest of the people to safety, and he was more determined than ever to accomplish it.

Fifty-Six

From where he was standing, Frank could see something shimmering at the far end of the huge chamber. He waved the group forward as he ran ahead to investigate. Emily went with him. There would be time enough to grieve the loss of their friend. Somehow, she felt certain now that they would return home soon. She felt sure that John would survive and had hope for their future.

When they arrived at the far wall, they came upon a gruesome discovery. There was another wide hallway to pass through before they could reach what Frank thought would be the machine they needed to open the portal. On each side of hall were large rooms, like storage bins crudely formed out of earth and stone. Each one was gated off by a metal grate that kept its gruesome contents from spilling out into the passageway. Bodies of humans and other creatures were stacked high inside the bin. Their faces were twisted. It appeared they had suffered terribly before they died.

"This is fucked up." Frank kept his voice low, perhaps out of respect for the dead, or maybe caution that there might yet be monsters lurking nearby. The stench was overwhelming as they walked through this passage. Emily struggled to keep from being sick, averting her eyes away from the piles of dead bodies as well as she could.

At the end of the hall stood the machine Frank was looking to find. It was similar to the one he had assembled from the plans contained in the scrolls they had taken from Iraq. This alien machine was much larger and seemed to be more intricately detailed. The crystals were longer than the ones he had used, and there were two more for a total of six. They appeared to be light and colorless like… diamonds?

Frank inspected the machine while Emily gathered her courage again. When she had seen the bodies of all of the people, she had begun to doubt that everything would be fine. Had she been a fool to think they would get back home?

The rest of the group had been following them at a distance and were now passing by the piles of corpses. Some became sick, dropping to their knees with dry heaves. Others gasped, crying out. This could have been their destiny. It was what had awaited them if the others had not arrived to rescue them.

As many of them that could squeeze through into the room with the machine now stood waiting for the next part of the plan to unfold. Fortunately, they were unaware that there was no plan. Like everything that had happened from the time the team had come to rescue them until the last battle in the chamber, there could be no plan, only the will of a few former soldiers and one fierce woman to fight for their survival.

When the room was nearly full, Max and Philip moved the overflow back out the hallway and into the large chamber to wait. It was too much to ask them to stand amongst the dead for any length of time. The stress of that experience alone might have finished off some of the weaker survivors.

Frank stood with his arms crossed, taking in the entire view of the enhanced machine. "We need to figure out how to turn this thing on. At my house, there were computers to control it, but I doubt there are any computers here. There must be some kind of control panel and a different kind of power source. Joe, get a couple of other people and help me look for them. Everybody else move back and give us some space." Frank immediately began searching around the machine for cables or anything that might lead to the control device.

While the others searched, Emily wondered at the two strange beings standing next to John like bodyguards and watching for any threat against him. The cat-men who had carried him were standing near the machine. They had carefully moved him to the side of the room and lowered him to the floor. Now they were standing guard over him as though he were one of their own. She approached them cautiously, speaking in a calm even voice so as not to startle them.

"How is he? Can you tell if he is getting any better?" She bent over him slowly, taking him by the hand and pressing her fingers to his wrist to check his pulse. "Thank God, he's still alive."

She knelt down to get a closer look, rubbing his arm and patting his hand in hopes of getting a response. She spoke softly into his ear. "Baby, you stay with me, you hear? We're almost out of this place. Just hold on." She bit her lip as she saw the blood that had seeped through the bandage that covered his wounds.

"Honey, I need to tell you, all that shit I gave you about Rachel… I knew you didn't have anything going on with her. I'm sorry I was just… I don't know, not jealous really… How stupid was that anyway? Hold on, okay? We're going to get back home and get you some help."

Suddenly, Emily had an idea. When she had turned on the beam from the sword, it had hit Archer and energized him somehow. It restored his health. Why hadn't she thought of this before?

She pulled the sword back out of her backpack and pointed it at John. Pressing her hand into the stone on the handle, the beam of light streamed from the sword and lit up John's chest. She held the beam steady for a few seconds and then took her hand off the stone. The glare from the bright beam in the dark room had temporarily blinded her and anyone standing nearby. Apologizing to those who did not realize how they had been blinded, she felt for the opening of her pack and slipped the sword back in for safekeeping.

"John? Can you hear me?" She reached out her hand and placed it gently on his chest. Touching his lips, she could tell that he was still unconscious. Nothing had changed from what she could tell. Obviously, the sword had no effect on the physical injuries of humans. She tried to manage her disappointment, telling herself that at least he was still alive. It gave her the hope she needed to continue.

Meanwhile the guys had finished searching every inch of the area surrounding the machine, but Frank didn't like the result, or lack thereof. There seemed to be no visible means of controlling the machine, and there was definitely no known power source. Joe continued looking it over, unwilling to give up.

As he marveled at the construction compared to the one back at Frank's lab, he found a slot and a sliding track that had been previously overlooked. The opening appeared made to fit some kind of a control knob or handle. To one side, there were ten evenly spaced notches, each one marked with a special character and a glyph of some type of animal. As he stared intently at the mechanism, the answer came to him.

"Frank, over here!" He motioned his friend to step around to the other side of the machine.

"What did you find?"

"If I ain't crazy, this looks like it's set up to control this thing somehow. I don't see any cables attached to it, but there's a slot there, so there must be some kinda key."

"It's larger than any key slot I've ever seen." Frank rubbed his hand over the track and looked closer at the carvings beside it. He looked around for anything obvious that would fit into the slot, but there was nothing nearby.

Meanwhile, Joe had stepped away to talk to Emily. When he returned, he was holding the sword in his hand. He was grinning wide as he held it up to Frank. "I used to use a screwdriver to start cars without a key when I was a kid." He turned his back to Frank and inserted the sword into the slot, pushing it in all the way in to the hilt.

"So how do we hit the gas pedal?" Frank asked.

"Put one hand on the handle, and use the other one to add a little pressure on the stone." Emily answered as she walked toward the men to get a better look.

Joe did as she suggested, taking hold of the sword and touching the stone with two of his fingers. The intense beam of light shot out from the sword and into the machine. There was an immediate response as it came to life, humming and vibrating as the light twisted through its components. It was amazing to see how it split into six separate bands and emerged from the other side, each band of color directed at a different crystal. The crystals began to glow with the light and color of the beam that fed into it.

"Looks like these crystals are storing energy, maybe saving up for a critical burst." Frank was becoming hopeful that they had found the secret to going home. The stone wall that was targeted by the machine was scorched from previous use. When at last the beams shot out from the diamonds, the wall began to shimmer as though melting.

"This thing is ready!" Frank yelled to the large group around him who were waiting, hoping to leave this world behind them.

Emily stepped forward and took Frank by the arm. "Listen, Frank, when we came through, we experienced a time shift. Remember? Seconds on our side are like minutes here. To make things more complicated, the portal we came through was constantly shifting. How do we know where this one will come out when we go through?"

The high-pitched sound coming from the machine got everyone's attention. They turned toward the source, and Emily's question was answered. The shimmering stone had dissolved as the wall became transparent.

"Look at that!" Phillip was pointing at the scene beyond the wall. "When we came through, we couldn't see what was on the other side, but here…"

Beyond the wall was a landscape as foreign to them as where they were standing. Unlike anything on earth, there was a glowing yellow mountain range rising into a blackened sky. Many multi-legged creatures scattered in front of the portal as though scrambling to get out of the way.

"What do you see?" Joe called out from his control position.

"Did you see any settings on the control panel, Joe? 'Cause I think we're looking at another world. From the looks of those creatures scurrying away, something big is coming our way." Frank sounded more than nervous.

"Oh, shit, yeah! There are some glyphs here. I didn't realize they were actual settings. Hang on!" He pushed in on the sword and slid it to the notch illustrated with a character he didn't recognize and an image resembling a man. The sound that was coming from the machine seemed to wind down before cranking up again, and the alien mountain scene faded away as the wall became stone again. When the portal opened again, the sight before them was agonizing and overwhelming.

"Oh… my… God." Emily gasped. For as far as they could see, there were piles of bodies and bones divided by a winding path.

"I guess this is some kind of dumping station for disposing of the dead." Frank stepped to one side to get a look at it from a different angle. He wanted to see what could be just around the corner of the trail. Perhaps this was the way out despite the gruesome scene. What he saw was even more horrifying. There were creatures as big as cows eating their way through the bodies. "Try another one Joe, and hurry," he yelled as he stepped back.

Once again the rippling surface of the stone appeared as Joe slid the sword to a new position. As the wall became transparent once more, the new view was dimly lit. As their eyes adjusted to the change, they could see another wall constructed of individual stones. It seemed to be a small room, or it could be a tunnel since the light seemed to come indirectly from both sides.

Frank didn't want to take a chance with his people. They could all pass through this gateway to find themselves crammed into a stone chamber like the one in Iraq with no visible exit. If that were to happen, and the portal moved, would they be able to return?

***

At such an early hour of the morning, the man jogging through the park was alert, choosing the safest path he knew. It was his second time around, and he had ten minutes to go before his workout was complete. When he rounded the bend, he could see the dark tunnel ahead of him. Here he was always cautious because the tunnel offered a perfect hiding place for anyone who might want to get the drop on him.

There was no one in sight as he neared the entrance. He slowed a bit to give himself time to check his surroundings. Seeing no signs of a threat, he gained confidence as he peered into the shadows and began to accelerate, jogging right through without incident until he heard the strange sound from behind.

***

Frank was trying to decide what they should do next when he saw a shadow moving off to the side. "Get ready to shut it down, Joe! Something is out there, and I can't see what it is."

He held his breath, waiting. This was it. If there was anything alien or threatening there, he was not certain they would be able close the portal in time. And, if so, they would still need to figure out this machine. Without the ability to decode the markings on the interface, they could be trapped in this hellish world. There was no time to dwell on it. Whatever was out there was nearly upon them.

Frank raised his weapon preparing to shoot anything threatening that might come through the portal. Everyone's nerves were frayed, and those nearest the portal braced themselves for another fight. As the jogger ran past, everyone exhaled at once. Although ridiculous in his lime green nylon shorts and his fishnet tank top, to Frank, that man screamed of home. "We're going home!" he shouted. "Hold that setting, Joe. I think we've got the right place."

Frank was overjoyed as he gave the directive. "Everyone listen, this is it! Get yourselves lined up, five or six across. After the first row of people step through, the next will count to ten before following them. Help the weak and injured get through first. Step slowly, but when you hit the ground on the other side, you'll need to run as fast as you can. Go in either direction. It's an open tunnel. Does everyone understand?"

Everyone at the front of the group nodded their heads and began lining up. The first row of six didn't need coaxing. They went through with no hesitation, and the others fell in behind them as they stepped through the portal. Row by row, everyone was smiling as the large group moved forward to get to the gateway.

Emily stepped over to where Frank was helping people through. She looked distressed. "Frank, I need to get John to a doctor."

"Of course, Emily, I should have thought of it. I'm sorry." He reached into his pocket. "Get him through and don't wait to call 911." He pulled his phone from his pocket and turned it on. "Thank God. The battery looks pretty good." He handed it to her.

"Once you are sure that help is on the way, call my lawyer, Quincy. You'll find him in my contacts list. Tell him that I need him to take care of these people. I want him to get them medical treatment and passage home. He'll ask you for the code. Tell him, *Carnival.*"

Emily took the phone, and Frank put his hand on her shoulder. "When he comes to, tell John I said thank you for coming after me, will ya?"

She nodded. "I will. You know there's nothing that could have prevented him from coming."

Frank smiled, "That's John, and the rest of them, too. Archer gave his life in the effort. Best damn team a man could ever lead. I'm honored to have known them all."

"Known? Frank, what are you saying?"

He looked out at the people walking slowly through the portal. "There are others here who need saving. God knows how many from what I understand. I'm gonna stay and help as many as I can, then I'll be back. You go now. Get John to a hospital."

Emily hugged him. "We'll see you on the other side then?" Her eyes welled up at the thought that he may never return from this new mission.

"Yes, Ma'am!" He snapped to attention and saluted her. "And Emily... you are one hell of an incredible woman and one of the best soldiers I have ever had the honor to serve with." Releasing his salute, he continued, "John is one lucky man."

She smiled, "He sure is! And I'm going to let him know about it." She turned away toward the group.

The cat-men who had been carrying John passed him to two of the stronger men. Emily joined them and did what she could to help support John. When they stepped through the portal, the blast of fresh air hit them like a wave, rushing over them as their bodies accelerated adjusting to the time difference. Some of the people who had already crossed over were confused and compressed into the small space in the tunnel.

"Move out of the tunnel," shouted Emily, reminding them that they were supposed to move away from the portal. "There are more coming out behind us!"

The survivors moved out from both sides of the stone archway to the surprise of a growing crowd of onlookers gathering in the area. As Emily tried to move away from the portal, more people came through bumping them from behind. The men carrying John struggled to keep their hold as they headed toward open ground.

She blinked as she emerged from the tunnel into the sunlight. It was a miracle to be back home in their world. Calling out to the locals gathered there, she asked, "Could someone please give us a hand? We have quite a few injured people here."

She guided the men carrying John toward an open area. "Where are we anyway?"

A woman holding her miniature poodle responded, "This is Central Park. You're in New York City."

Fifty-Seven

An army of police, firefighters, and paramedics descended on Central Park that morning. Before the first wave of survivors had been cleared or dispatched to local hospitals, several hundred more came through the portal. City officials closed the park to allow the FBI to investigate, but the enormity of the event made it impossible to keep a few determined reporters from slipping through. More than one helicopter flew overhead.

The local hospitals were overwhelmed by the sudden rush of starving and dehydrated victims. Those who had been treated for minor injuries were asked to remain until they could be interviewed by law enforcement officials. It was no small feat to make room to contain the people waiting to be debriefed.

As the second wave of survivors finished pouring into the park, two men came through the portal and slipped away undetected. Frank and Joe had completed their mission with the assistance of the strange cat creatures. When they last saw their alien friends, they were gingerly handling a remote control device wired to explosive charges, ready to destroy the machine.

The two exhausted men quickly distanced themselves from the park, seeking out the first fast food restaurant they could find. They ate until they couldn't take another bite. As they walked down the street finishing their giant-sized drinks, Frank stopped at a nearby kiosk to pick up a new phone.

After making some calls, they headed for the airport. The remaining members of the team were located by security personnel and told to meet them at the airport for the flight home. Except for John and Emily, the team would be flying back to San Francisco, first class.

Frank's attorney made arrangements for all of the people they had rescued. Their medical expenses were covered, loved ones contacted, and airline tickets arranged. By the time Frank's chartered plane had landed, many of the survivors were already on their way home.

Meanwhile, John lay unconscious connected to tubes and monitors. It seemed he had been injected with an unidentified poison, the result of the bite he had sustained in the fight with the Cyclops. Emily made no effort to explain what had happened. She simply told the medical personnel that he had been bitten and that when she found him, he had already passed out.

She had not left his side, and had barely slept as she waited for his recovery. The doctors assured her that he would survive. Hoping that he would do better than survive, she prayed there would be no permanent damage. Early in the morning of the third day, she was awakened by the sound of John's voice. He was talking to someone, telling the story of their adventure. Describing where they had been, he told as much as he could remember about what had happened.

"John, honey, you're awake!" She stood, moving to kiss him on the forehead. "Who were you talking to?"

"Hi, babe. Sorry we woke you up. You looked so beautiful, sleeping over there. I was talking to Warren here." He motioned toward the empty chair next to his bed. "He was telling me about the heinous accident that landed him in this joint, and I was telling him about *our* little visit to Neverland." He looked over at his visitor.

"John… who? There's no one there." She put her hand to his forehead to see if he had a fever. As she reached for the call button to fetch the nurse, he put his hand on hers and stopped her. He turned to look at the man who was grinning at him now. John looked back at Emily. She was staring at him with concern.

As John turned to ask his guest to say something so Emily could hear, John realized what was happening. Now, he could see what he hadn't before. There was a large section of skull missing from the back of the man's head and bits of brain matter hung down from the open wound. The hair surrounding the fatal injury was matted with dried blood.

"Oh shit, Em!" John gulped and turned pale, as he looked at her wide-eyed. "What was it that kid said in that movie? I see…"

"Dead people." She finished the sentence with him.

Also Available From J.H. Glaze:
The Paranormal Adventures of John Hazard:
The Spirit Box – Book I
NorthWest – Book II
Send No Angel – Book III
Ghost Wars – Book IV (coming soon)

The Life We Dream – Novella
Forced Intelligence – Novella
The Horror Challenge Volumes I, II, III

RUNE – A Serial Novel

Books by JH Glaze Can Be Found On Most Book Retail
Web Sites In eBook or Paperback Editions.

Follow JH Glaze on Facebook
Twitter: @themostcoolone
Website www.JHGlaze.com
Goodreads.com

Thank You For Reading!

Made in the USA
Columbia, SC
16 November 2024

46688255R00159